As a Decade Fades

JOSHUA FIELDS MILLBURN

Asymmetrical Press
Missoula, Montana

Published by Asymmetrical Press.

Some of the profits garnered from the sale of this book will likely be spent on shit I don't need, although I'll do my best to refrain.

The stories in this book are fiction. All names, characters, places, and events are imaginary. Where the names of actual celebrities or corporate entities are used, they're used for fictional purposes and do not constitute assertions of fact. No resemblance to anyone or anything real is intended nor should it be inferred. So if you think this book is about you, you're wrong.

Library of Congress Cataloging-in-Publication Data
As a decade fades / Joshua Fields Millburn — 2nd ed.
Print ISBN: 978-1-938793-02-8
eISBN: 978-1-938793-03-5
WC: 65,183
1. Author. 2. Title. 3. Loneliness. 4. Death. 5. Music.

Feel free to take pieces of this book and replicate them online or in print, but please link back to joshuafieldsmillburn.com. If you want to use more than a few paragraphs, please email themins@themins.com.

Cover photo by Adam Dressler
Author photo by Joshua Weaver
Cover design by Dave LaTulippe

Author info:
Author: joshuafieldsmillburn.com
Essays: theminimalists.com

ASYM METR ICAL

For Keri.

The years go by / a decade fades
A love don't die / it just grows with age

—Trent Dabbs
"New Morning"

as a decade fades

Are you sure you want to do this?

PART ONE || **Brooklyn**

SOMEONE TO REST THIS WEIGHT ON

Things could have been worse. But not much worse.

Jody Grafton stood a few feet from his empty bed, multitasking, getting a Marlboro going with his right hand while the fingers on his callused left separated the thin aluminum blinds covering his window. Outside: snow, whitewashed sky, the sun anchored to the heavens like a spotlight over a cold and brilliant one-man hell.

The telephone rang again. It had been ringing all morning. The name on the caller ID was always the same. Jody finally surrendered to the noise, picked up the receiver without a word. Silence answered for him.

"Hello? Jody?" Her voice reached through the phone; its modest panic turned him on. Not sexually, but in a way that stroked his ego. He wasn't sure why, but it excited him to know that she needed him more than he needed her.

"Jody, are you there?"

There was an extended silence.

"Hello?" she asked again.

"Whadda you want?" He conceded these few words, dragging his consonants in a Midwestern fashion, his voice dressed in smoke and early morning wine. He hadn't spoken with her in weeks, not since she'd nearly had him arrested in that snow-covered Taco Bell parking lot. He thought the only way to keep her at bay now was to remain cold and yet somehow show her he cared. It was a strange dichotomy. People don't know how to love the ones they love until they disappear from their lives. The clouds through the window formed a discord of patterns, a perfect white motif, beautiful only from a great distance, because if he were to get any closer the clouds would lose their beauty, turning more and more into a foggy haze the closer he got. But they were perfect from afar—the homes of angels. So he kept his distance.

"What do I want? What do I want!" she shouted through the phone. "What do you mean, what do I want?"

A tense silence returned to the line.

"I'm pregnant."

OUT OF THE STORM

Paste Magazine
January 28, 2006
Review by Rebbecca McCulla
★★★★★ 5/5 Stars

Ohio-based singer-songwriter Jody Grafton drinks from the same wellspring as innumerable other contemporary American crooners. But his music bears little resemblance to anything on the radio. Adept at merging folk and rock influences with decaffeinated chords and somber, poetic lyrics, Grafton mines the fertile seams between life's emotional and intellectual realms.

On his second full-length album, *Out of the Storm* (Geffen/Interscope), Grafton explores further than his previous effort by stripping away the excess, leaving only the essential. He does so with good company in tow, enlisting support from an unlikely trio of African-American fellow Ohioans: Eric Wallace (bass guitar), Michael Emerson (drums, piano), and Evan Howard (pedal-steel, electric guitar). Even Grafton's wife, Kelly, a high school music teacher, contributes cello and violin to several tracks. Out front, Grafton is an unrefined acoustic fingerpicker with the road-weathered voice of a Zen folksinger, narrating gritty tales suffused with equal parts hope and despair.

The lyrics alone make *Out of the Storm* a

serious contender for singer-songwriter album of the year. "Her eyes were filled with raindrops / am I the one to blame? / Did I love her more last summer / eight months before the rain?" Grafton ponders in his unique, grating baritone on "Rain Without Lightning." He digs deeper on "Meaning of Life": "Another rearview mirror / leaving so much left undone / Never said goodbye / another song goes unsung."

Grafton's music is a quietly brilliant mixture of poetry and prose whittled down to a doleful perfection that reflects the region from which he hails: unpretentious, under-ambitious, beautifully oppressed — not unlike the empty factories and vacant buildings that pepper the cityscape of his hometown. Grafton himself is a young man with an old soul, wise beyond his years. *Out of the Storm* is contemporary and timeless, raw and full of life, gritty and staggeringly beautiful, leaving the listener yearning only for an encore.

A RADICALLY ATTENUATED HISTORY OF GENERATION X

From across the restaurant table she smiled at him, or perhaps through him, and swallowed a sip of wine from her second glass and waited for him to hurl a compliment or witticism in her direction. He was leaving town the following morning, uncertain of when he would return. Uneasy cunctation filled the atmosphere nearest their table, suspended in the crosshairs of their evening together. She was so distracted by what he thought of her—by what *everybody* thought—that all her own thoughts were merely carefully considered rebuttals to his internalized criticisms of her, which criticisms were purely her own unconscious assimilations of his (potentially non-existent) internalized views. She sensed that her rebuttals—should she ever be forced to articulate them—adequately illustrated his faults while simultaneously abdicating her of hers: it was obvious to her that her lust for money and puissance and material possessions and physical attractiveness and sexual prowess (and something else she could not name but nonetheless searched endlessly and aimlessly for) was negated by his desire for sex and personal status and goal attainment and achievement and more sex and public acknowledgment and eminence and individual conquest and even more sex (and some other unnamed thing he wasn't able to identify and was at a loss to locate no matter where he searched). And among the masticatory sounds of the restaurant she examined the air for fragments of validation that would justify her thoughts, while on the other side of the table he brushed an invisible piece of lint from his shirt with his right hand, thinking of tomorrow and hoping the date would end well that night. And yet they never found what they were looking for, and so their search continued—a target without a bullseye.

LEAPING INTO THE UNKNOWN

Rolling Stone Magazine
January 28, 2006
Review by Ryan Noble
★★★★☆ 4/5 Stars

"Lie by me / we can be alone together / Lie to me / we can believe these lies forever," sings Jody Grafton on the title track of his second album, *Out of the Storm*, the appropriately titled follow-up to his impressive but commercially unsuccessful debut, *Into the Storm*. Grafton, a 24-year-old singer-songwriter from Dayton, Ohio, caught the attention of mainstream radio stations with his haunting break-up ballad, "Ohio Again," late last year. The staggering success of that song quickly turned Grafton into an artist from whom we wanted to hear more.

His sandpaper baritone conjures the ghosts of a younger, grimmer Bob Dylan, while his cold, dispirited lyrics leave the listener with chills that bond them to every song. The music manifests itself in the words much more than the melodies; the twelve-track album is light in instrumentation but heavy in the melancholy-laden prose of a gifted new songwriter.

If there's a downside to this new album, it's its immense darkness — a darkness that seems to repel all light. Never has a songwriter conveyed loneliness the same way Grafton does on his lowest days. Not a single song feels redemptive or hopeful; the album is marked by sadness, longing, and abandonment, though we get the idea that Grafton wasn't attempting to cheer anyone up with this record. The album lingers in states of the emotionally downtrodden as he leaves the happy songs to lazy pop stars.

Out of the Storm's most striking moment might be on "I Won't Be There When You're Alone," an invitation to leap into the unknown. It's just Grafton and his guitar accompanied by a mystical piano/violin combo; the melody revels in hardhearted ache, the lyrics are at once reassuring and alarming: "Can't do this forever / I don't love you anymore." Maybe it's about a loved one, maybe it's about the pangs of endless touring, maybe it's about suicide. Half the allure is in not knowing.

IT'S ALL SO QUIET IN BROOKLYN

Jody Grafton had no taste for the day's potential. He waited to board a plane and leave behind everything he'd broken, everything he'd left undone, trying to untangle himself from a decade of dilemma, if only for a while. Maybe he had to go away to come back.

From among the serpentine security line, he watched a symphony of emotions take place just beyond the faux-velvet ropes: a soldier in full uniform embraced his young wife, meeting and kissing and holding his son for the first time; a man in a suit and striped tie with a smart four-in-hand knot was greeted by another man in a cheaper suit holding a sign with the first man's last name on it; a prepubescent daughter darted past the other pedestrians and yelled "Daddy!" and embraced her father with a hug that conveyed a tenderness on which many Hollywood movie plots are predicated; a cacophony of crying babies echoed down an out-of-sight terminal somewhere past the metal detectors; a mother hugged her boy and cried and hugged her boy again and kissed him on the forehead as he bent down, bidding him farewell and wishing him a safe trip to his new college a thousand miles away; a man in his seventies was welcomed by a greeting party of no one at all, and his cold stare couldn't mask the grim awareness on his face. The old man bypassed the crowded luggage carousel and exited the airport's large automatic doors into the waterlogged Ohio air. The overhead parking-lot lights extinguished themselves and the early morning sun illuminated the old man's trek to the long-term parking garage, casting shadows indiscriminately on everything that was beautiful and everything that was not.

Jody unlaced and slipped off his Redwing boots and placed them in a plastic bin alongside his duffle bag and guitar case on the X-ray machine's conveyor belt. He forgot to remove his own belt and so the machine beeped when he walked through the metal detector. A burly woman in a tight security-guard uniform with epaulets, wearing a name tag that proved that her first name was the same as Jody's, waited for him, holding a wand on the other side of the metal detector. She looked him over in an effort to establish his merits and noticed the tattoos on both arms and asked him whether he had any piercings in an accusatory and assuming tone that seemed to project annoyance or boredom or somehow both at the same time.

Jody thought about telling her that his scrotum was pierced (even though it wasn't) but decided against it before the words left his mouth. "Nope. No piercings."

"Anything in your pockets?"

"No. They're empty. Whaddabout my belt buckle?" He lifted his shirt, exposing his thin midriff and the light blond hairs on his stomach and a leather belt looped through his jeans.

"You're supposed to remove your belt before you enter the metal detector."

"I'll make a note of that."

She used her wand to check the rest of his person for weapons or bombs or additional belt buckles.

"You know, if they ever catch Osama Bin Laden, they shouldn't kill him or put him in prison," Jody said. "They should make him go through airport security over and over and over."

She didn't find this funny, although the guy collecting his things from the conveyor belt in front of him laughed out loud and repeated the joke to his wife.

Jody slipped his boots back on, grabbed his stuff, and headed toward terminal C. He was the only person at the airport wearing sunglasses indoors. Although he didn't know it, he looked like a songwriter. Even without the guitar case, it was his root identity: black Ray-Bans low on the bridge of his nose, ostensibly camouflaging either a cocaine high and/or a black eye; a white V-neck teeshirt exposing the top of a crown tattoo on his chest; the colorful sleeve tattoo on his right arm and the word FREEDOM in large calligraphy on his left; the leather boots he'd worn for years, real shitkickers on which daylight might reveal flecklets of dried blood; and a facial expression that said he just might kick your ass, just for the hell of it. A nonchalant rocker, not like the dozens of posers you saw at rock concerts, all of whom tried too hard to *look* the part with their skinny jeans, their tufts of longish hair, their thin suspenders, their idiotic painted fingernails. No, Jody appeared to be a genuine rockstar, one whose name was on the tip of your tongue but it escaped you and you weren't able to place him: "Aren't you, um … ?" or "Didn't you play in … ?"

"Flight 214 to LaGuardia will be boarding in a few minutes," a chipper, annoying voice called over the loudspeaker.

Jody sat near the gate and fiddled with the pen Jolene had given him just before they said their awkward goodbyes in the airport lobby. Overhead, President Obama was suspended from the ceiling, speaking through multiple television monitors. He had aged at least five years during his first eighteen months in office. Jody ignored the president's words and continued to fuss with Jolene's pen.

The word UNFORGETTABLE, the title of the old Nat King Cole song—*their* song—was engraved on the pen's stainless-steel shaft. It had become *their* song almost jokingly at first. They'd first heard it around 2 a.m. piped through the Muzak speakers of a twenty-four-hour superstore less than a week into their relationship. Jody sang and danced awkwardly up and down the aisles, joshing around and doing his best to imitate Cole's confident swagger under the hideously bright fluorescent lights as they searched the store for a late-night snack and a box of condoms and something that might resemble happiness. He didn't know all the words to the later verses, but that didn't matter; Jolene was still captivated by the way he sang the song to her, his raspy voice not unlike Cole's. They heard the song once more two days later at a diner, again late at night, when Jolene romantically declared it "their song" without a hint of sarcasm or irony. It took Jody all his strength not to mock her. And thus it had been *their* song over the past eight months. Eight months of on-again off-again goodbyes and crying. Eight months of breakup sex and makeup sex and just plain old regular sex when the other varieties of sex weren't necessary. Eight months seemed to be a threshold for Jody, something abortive about it, always a hairsbreadth short of carrying a meaningful relationship to term, going through all the pain and agony of developing a bond, one that could *almost* live on its own, before inserting a coat hanger and ending it gruesomely. And nearly every relationship ended this way, except one, which lasted almost eight years, and was more like slaughtering a child you loved while looking in her eyes.

Why the hell did she give me a pen? He felt the grooves of the word with his thumbnail and wondered if he scratched at the first two letters long enough would the pen instead say FORGETTABLE, and if it did would that somehow alter anything in the real world? *Is she thinking of me?* was the question he caught himself asking, even though that was a stupid question: he knew she was, especially after he felt her belly the day before—nothing more than a nub, at four months she wasn't yet showing and he didn't feel any movement, which meant it might not be real, right? She said she was going to keep it, and he knew he was selfish for asking her to reconsider and for saying he would be there for her before he kissed her on her forehead at the airport gate and tears streamed down her face, because they both knew that he wouldn't. She was unsure when he would come back to Ohio. He hadn't purchased a ticket for a return flight. People don't know how to love the ones they love until they disappear from their lives.

The airplane had ashtrays in the armrests and "no smoking" signs overhead, which Jody thought of as a suitable metaphor for much of his own life. Often he would create something—a relationship, a connection, a memory—just to make it unusable, not allowing himself full access to himself, placing barriers around the intangibles he had created. Would he do the same thing with a child? He was unsure, although he was certain he didn't want a child. Not because he couldn't handle it or because he was selfish, but because he knew it was unfair—unfair to the child and to the mother and perhaps to the entire world for him to create something that was half of him, half of which was broken, which meant at best the child would be one-quarter despoiled and this seemed unfair to the world and everyone in it.

Before take-off the plane's engines sang of the work involved in propelling a large heap of metal into the sky. Jody helped a large woman lift her large backpack into the overhead storage compartment. It barely fit and they were forced to wedge the backpack and slam the lid several times before the latch held it in place. Then a pretty girl gave him the death stare as he settled into 13C in the last row. She told him scornfully that *he* was in *her* seat. But he wasn't. It turned out that she was assigned to 13B, directly beside him (but appreciably farther from the pungent smells of the lavatory). After realizing her error and apologizing profusely, she became more friendly and talkative throughout the flight, which seemed to annoy the passengers for several rows in every direction. Even the woman with a crying baby in front of them looked irritated. Jody reveled in everyone's indignation; their shared discontent made this girl tolerable. She said her name was Carolina ("Like the states!") but then told him she went by Kendra. Jody didn't bother to ask why. He didn't care whether it was her middle name or some weird nickname or maybe she had changed her name haphazardly, trying to escape a previous identity, trying to run away from a past none of us can run away from, a past we can choose only to ignore.

Kendra was twenty, she told Jody. She reminded him of someone who was in the midst of rebelling against her conservative parents. Her outfit consisted of a leopard-print cardigan, a pink spandex undershirt, and black full-length tights. She was toting an oddly embellished wicker purse filled with cheap 8½" x 11" picture frames—the kind of frames a person buys at Walmart for a dollar. There were no pictures in the frames and she carried no other luggage. Long straight hair covered her head; Jody liked the way it fell in her face. She slipped off her white canvas shoes five minutes into the flight and remained barefoot for the duration. She had tiny feet. An involuntary glance revealed no ring on her left hand, not that he expected to see one on this girl. There wasn't a ring on his finger either, not since last fall, not since before Jolene.

Between chunks of trivial conversation with Kendra, Jody thumbed through a few pages of the in-flight magazine. Kendra said that she refused to fly with any other airline because of the fresh-baked chocolate-chip cookies this airline offered on every flight. She raved over this apparent extravagance like a paid spokeswoman, but after the flight attendant handed Jody a cookie, Kendra declined the offer for one herself, stating she didn't like chocolate-chip cookies. When she spoke, there was no regional accent to place her. She said she was from Provo, Utah, but Jody sensed she might be lying. A strange thing to lie about. Perhaps she was running from someone or something. Eventually their conversation fizzled out, as conversations do, as people move on in their own direction, living a life that briefly intersected with yours.

Jody looked out the window. The clouds didn't seem like clouds at all, more like bothersome, dense fog. They lost their wonderment at this height. The flight attendant brought him a small plastic cup filled with orange juice and eight ice cubes. Jody had a habit of counting things without realizing he was counting. He counted seventeen people who used the undersized restroom next to him, most of whom were puzzled by its door, which opened like a kitchen pantry's folding door. It wasn't the folding part that confused them though; most people simply couldn't locate the handle on the door, and so they pushed and pulled and sometimes punched or kicked the door until they figured it out. Sometimes the easiest things in life are the hardest and most frustrating things to understand.

They landed at LaGuardia three minutes past noon. A fast, smooth landing as far as landings go. The plane taxied, Jody waited. Besides the crew, he was the last person to deplane.

The tarmac smelled like gasoline and humidity. A slightly disheveled Hasidic Jew, whom Jody mistook for an Amish man, said hello to him at the bottom of the stairs as he deplaned.

He hadn't checked any luggage so he didn't need to wait with the masses at the conveyor belt. A song called "She Likes Girls" played through Jody's headphones as he maneuvered LaGuardia's infinite hallways, exited the airport lobby, lit a cigarette, and waited for his bus to arrive.

The sun broke through the clouds and the heat intensified. The dense New York air clung to his body. His skin nearly sizzled in the sunlight and he knew he was an idiot for smoking in this heat. But much like the rest of his life, he couldn't help himself.

The bus was late. Jody leaned on a concrete pole; above his head was a sign warning everyone that it was against the law to smoke within 50 feet of an entrance to the building. He took a long drag from his cigarette and never once looked up at the sign. It was so humid that even the cigarette felt waterlogged. He inhaled water vapor and nicotine and exhaled a damp plume. All the bench seats were full, so dozens of people stood near the seating area. Everyone avoided eye contact. Sometimes a crowded place can feel the most alone.

When his bus finally arrived, everyone cleared the bench and entered before him. There was standing room only by the time he boarded.

He wasn't sure when it had happened, but one day he woke up halfway between somewhere and nowhere and he was suddenly twenty-something and nearing thirty as the decade faded. And now he was broke and alone, traveling to New York with not much more than a guitar and a thousand dollars in his pocket, plus a pregnant girlfriend he didn't love waiting at home. The tightrope that was his life's path had slacked, but somehow he hadn't fallen. Making it big (again) in the Big City wasn't the way he'd imagined it would happen, especially at this late stage.

He had already been through all of it before during the last decade: the awful venues of his early twenties, playing night after night to drunken crowds who paid him less attention than he paid them; the sleeping at rest areas along Interstate Whatever in Kansas or Iowa or Indiana; the bigger gigs, opening for mediocre semi-famous acts with too many guitars; the shitty record deal at age twenty-two, followed by a better record deal a year later; the second album and the hit song at twenty-four, a song he hated by now but everyone wanted him to sing and so he obliged; the national tour accompanying that record; the scores of women he turned down in city after city, remaining faithful not because of love but out of a pious sense of loyalty; and the pain of not making another successful album or hit song and at twenty-seven, losing the record deal and the income and any glimmer of pseudo-fame he might have had for that brief snapshot of time. The faster it came, the faster it went.

And so now he had to try once more. This was his only remaining option: trying, searching for meaning. But maybe there was no meaning at all, not to any of this. *Was there such a thing as a* mid-*mid-life crisis?* It's lonely at the top, but it's crowded and miserable at the bottom.

He stood near the front of the bus to Brooklyn, and

eventually, after the bus regurgitated a handful of patrons at its first three stops, a seat opened up next to a girl who had been looking out the window the entire ride. Except now, upon closer inspection, it appeared as though she was looking *at* the window, not beyond it. Jody sat next to her and removed his sunglasses for the first time in hours. Her gaze broke from the window; she wore the polite smile of a child with caring parents who could afford braces and regular dental visits—the type of girl who wouldn't've known his name had they gone to high school together, but for some reason, a decade later, these same women found him attractive and mysterious and "interesting." But of course they couldn't see what was inside. This girl looked trusting and innocent, like pictures of Jody's mother from her twenties—petite, fiercely gorgeous without effort. Her demeanor said she wasn't from New York but was comfortable here, wearing the great stain of experience, as if it wasn't her first time in the Big City. Jody pushed his duffle bag underneath the seat in front of him and stood his guitar case in the aisle.

"Do you play?" she asked. She was wearing a white summer dress and piercing green eyes and carried nothing on her person. She smelled like something sweet.

"I play a lot of things," he said.

She let out an amused sigh. "The guitar," she pointed at the case standing next him. Her accent was a New England accent, one with the broad A, so *guitar* sounded like *ga-TAH*, but it wasn't as blatant as in the movies.

"What, this? No I just carry this around so beautiful girls will ask me if I play guitar."

"Really? How's that working out for you?"

"Today's my first day, so I'd say pretty good."

"Oh yeah?"

"Yeah. I'm Jody, by the way. It's nice to meet you." He extended a hand.

"Michelle," she took his hand and held it for an extra fraction of a second. Her vision borrowed his; he knew those eyes and what they said: she thought she recognized him from somewhere but couldn't recall where. "So, are you a musician?"

"I write songs."

"What kind of songs?"

"If I wrote a song about you it would be a hit."

Her grin said she knew it was a cheesy line, but she couldn't keep herself from blushing.

"'I Love Everything You Are.' That's what I'd call it," he said.

"That's the silliest thing I've ever heard anyone say," she said but with a smile that said *thank you*.

"Thanks, *Mah*-shell." He sounded out her name as if he could taste both syllables. "I'll take that as a compliment."

"My friends call me Shelly."

"I'd like to be your friend, so I'll call you Shelly too."

She spoke ordinary words, but he felt those words could heal him, and for a moment the rest of the bus and its passengers and the world outside didn't exist. He didn't know why he did this to himself, but lust presented itself like ocean waves: it crashed and enveloped him, swallowed him whole, overwhelmed him with the prospect of having her. Oh what it would be like to kiss her and taste her soft tongue, to see her naked and feel the rush of her skin, his callused hands on the nape of her neck, her shoulders and tits and stomach, wanting every part of her body, inch by inch, diving in her beauty, planting his thumbs on her

23

hipbones and pressing his mouth to her thighs and working his way north with his tongue, making her tremble with pleasure, and then making love to her, entangled in the sheets for hours, coming together in unison. He envisioned the sight of his condom's post-orgasmic victory lap, swirling around the toilet bowl in triumphant celebration.

"Your accent. Are you from Boston?" he asked.

"Ohio, actually. But my family is from Rhode Island."

"Ohio? *I'm* from Ohio. Just got in today. What part?"

"I live in a small town just outside Columbus."

"No kidding. I'm like an hour from Columbus. You grew up in Ohio?"

"Sort of. We moved there when I was a teenager. My dad's job."

"So what brings you to New York?" Jody was still thinking about her tangled in the sheets with him. He usually ignored women, letting them make any necessary advances, but now he caught himself asking silly questions, questions like *So what brings you to New York?*

"I'm meeting a couple of girlfriends for the week in Brooklyn. We went to NYU together. Graduated like six years ago."

"Wait, that can't be true."

"What can't be true?"

"You just said you graduated from *college* six years ago?"

"Yeah. So?"

"That would make you like, what, twenty-nine then? And you are clearly *not* twenty-nine." It sounded like he was trying to flatter her, and maybe he was a little, but his skepticism was sincere. She looked nineteen and innocent in her angelic white dress. Was it possible to make it through your twenties so physically unscathed? If it's our experience that ages us, then she must have spent her twenties with nothing but lovely experiences, a balmy decade of bliss and benediction.

"Thanks but it's true."

"I'm going to need to see two forms of I.D., ma'am," he said in his best highway-trooper voice, a rural twang in it.

She seemed amused by everything he said, taking it all in, listening with the precision of a predator.

"OK. I'll buy it—for now at least. So you're traveling to Brooklyn all by yourself?"

"Yes. That's right."

"What part of Brooklyn do they live in? Bed-Stuy?" he asked, jokingly referencing of Brooklyn's relatively dangerous Bedford-Stuyvesant neighborhood, which had been the cultural center for the borough's black population for decades.

"I don't know the name of their neighborhood, but I don't even know what Bellsty is."

"*Bed*-Stuy. Home of Biggie Smallz and Jay-Z and various other rappers whose names I don't know," he said. "Anyway, I hope you're packing heat."

"Does pepper spray count as *heat*?"

"If it gets in my eye it counts."

"That's what she said," she said, eliciting Jody's first laugh of the day.

"You know, if you *were* going to Bed-Stuy then we'd be going to the same neighborhood."

"I see. So you can go to the dangerous part of town all by yourself, but it's too far-fetched for me to go?"

"I'm not sure if you've looked in a mirror lately, but my being there is infinitely more plausible than your being there."

"What are you talking about? I'm tough!" She was fair-skinned and tiny and thin—a foot shorter than Jody and not much more than a hundred pounds—but she had the confidence of a larger woman. She flexed her left bicep mockingly, and as she did her elbow crashed into the window and made a loud crack when it ricocheted off the glass.

"Ouch!" She looked embarrassed.

"You OK?"

"I'm fine," she said with a red-faced laugh.

"Point taken. You *are* tough."

"Shut up." She rubbed the pain out of her arm. "Are you staying in New York for long?"

"Not sure—haven't figured that out yet. You?"

"I'll be here for a week. Then I have to go back to Ohio and go back to work."

The bus ride was long, but it didn't feel long to Jody. Shelly got off two stops before he did. She needed to catch a train that would take her to an entirely different part of Brooklyn, but not before he got her number and gave her his and invited her to his friend Michael's show in Manhattan on Friday, writing down those details on the same piece of paper as his phone number. Before she got off the bus she told him she enjoyed riding next to him and assured him they would get together soon, and she said to call her whenever he wanted. He looked at the number. Her handwriting was sloppy, carefree. She smiled one last time, revealing those years of orthodontic craftsmanship, and he told her he would call.

Jody got off the bus and used Michael's directions to get to Bed-Stuy. Based on those directions he took the E train the wrong way, exited at 14th Street, boarded a new E train to Sutphin Boulevard, which connected to the J train that he rode too far to Broadway Junction and then took another J train past the Marcy Project buildings back to Gates Avenue where he got off and started walking the five blocks to Michael's brownstone apartment.

He was looking forward to seeing his old friend, looking forward to writing music together too. Michael had a great voice —much better than Jody's own limited range, and he was quite competent with an acoustic guitar—but he couldn't write songs like Jody. Half the reason he flew to New York was to see Michael—to watch his first big show and help him write some songs for his first album—and the other half was to get away from everything that was broken, start anew, find a way to get it right this time.

Jody started to sweat from his five-block trek. Damn, it was hot, nearly a hundred degrees, ninety-five percent relative humidity. He rounded the corner to Putnam Avenue and noticed Michael's buzz-cut head and stalky frame walking away from his apartment with a tattered, overfilled laundry bag hoisted over his shoulder.

"Mikey!" he yelled from half a block away.

Michael turned around, dropped the laundry bag. "Jody! What up!"

"What's up, man. Nice shirt," he said. Michael was wearing a crossing-guard-orange teeshirt with WANT A MUSTACHE RIDE? typeset below a large caricature of Tom Selleck. He had on black track pants and flip-flops and looked like he could be Laurence Fishburne's long-lost nephew: dark skinned, rugged, unshaven, unapologetic. And yet he was as kind and caring and sincere as anyone Jody knew.

Michael looked down at his shirt and then up at Jody and sported a big grin. They shook hands, embracing in a half-hug in the process. "Yeah, you know, I made sure I was looking real *purdy* for you," Michael faked a stereotypical hillbilly accent.

"I can tell. Where you headed?"

"Where do you think?" he said, picking up the laundry bag as evidence. "This might look like a bag of clothes, but it's actually filled with hundreds. I'm headed to the casino, son! Care to join me?" Michael loosened the laundry bag's drawstring and took an exaggerated whiff of its contents. "Smells like winning."

"Gross. Can I put my stuff in your apartment first? I'm sweating my ass off."

"Yeah, come on."

They walked three flights of stairs to apartment 3L. Jody had met Michael five years earlier during Jody's ascent to second-rate music-industry prominence. Michael had grown up in the neighborhood next to his, and they'd gotten to know each other the same way any semi-serious musicians in southwest Ohio got to know each other: they played scads of the same crummy venues over the years, rotating through odious bars and nightclubs and concert halls and restaurants and every other place young musicians played in their early years (and in their later years too, at least for the ones who never made it but still held on to their broken dreams of the Holy Trinity of rockstardom: the sad, empty desire for "fame, money, and women"). Over the years they funneled through places like South Park Tavern, Canal Street, Savoy, Blind Bob's, Holiday Inn Ballroom B, and dozens of other spots. Back then, at twenty-one, Michael had seemed so young, but he was already a talented musician, known on the local scene as a guy who could sing and play just about any instrument you put in front of him. Jody and Michael saw each other more and more as they cycled through their gigs, and in time Jody asked him to play drums on his second album, for which the record company paid him a meager $2,000 (the few backup vocals he provided for the album were gratis). A year later Michael and two other local musicians —Michael's roommate Evan and Jody's best friend Eric— accompanied Jody on his one and only headlining tour, a tour they affectionally dubbed the Jody and Three Black Guys Tour, the four of them cramming into their "tour bus" (a rented van) and dreaming that this was the start of something big for them, something special, a foundation on which they could build their musical careers and feed their creative ambitions and soon indulge in the fame and money and women they all so desperately sought, not knowing that this tour might be the zenith of their musical careers, and that any minuscule morsels of the Holy Trinity culminating from those shows might be *the day* they talked about when they talked about *back in the day* the way everyone reminisces about the past and talks about *back in the day*, yearning for a return to certainty, a return to a familiar place, a place to which they could never back, since the past does not equal the future and only the present determines the prospect of what lies ahead.

Before them stretched a day without prospect, accented by Brooklyn's summertime mugginess. The hellfire of the laundromat was first preceded by some obligatory catching-up at Michael's apartment. Neither of Michael's roommates were home, and even with the fan perched in the window it was at least ten degrees hotter than outside. Jody set his duffle and guitar in the livingroom and sat on the futon next to Michael and lit a cigarette and tried to recollect the sequence of events of the last two years since their tour: his third album, which seemed to be a stillbirth of an effort on the part of his record company; his being dropped from the label; his exit from playing music;

his mother's death; his marriage's final days; his subsequent failed relationships; his months of depression and drinking; his pregnant girlfriend; and, most recently, his newfound need to give music one last try (he omitted February's failed suicide attempt).

Michael listened attentively and offered standard words of encouragement, sincere niceties a friend often needs to hear from another friend. Michael's servile interlocutor lightened the mood, freeing Jody from his memories. Michael was mostly unchanged by the past two years. He had put on maybe fifteen pounds, but he looked good, healthy, jovial. He made small talk about his music and about how New York girls differed from Ohio girls and yet how all girls were all essentially the same in the end. They both peppered in mindless comments regarding the heat, and they both complained that Michael didn't have air conditioning so they couldn't escape the summer.

The apartment was a travesty. There were remnants of a missing roommate who had moved out unannounced two weeks prior, all his things scattered into makeshift piles in one corner of the livingroom: recording equipment, DVDs, CDs, clothes, a pair of shoes, a single flip-flop, a deflated basketball, garbage bags filled with god-knows-what. Many of these things Michael and his roommates intended to sell in an effort to cover the AWOL roommate's portion of the rent.

As the heat somehow turned even more unbearable, they evacuated the apartment for the laundromat a few blocks away, walking past rows of brownstone houses in various stages of decay. Scores of people sat on their stoops smoking cigarettes and yelling at their children, skin baking in the summer sun, although they didn't seem to mind the searing temperatures. The street smelled the way garbage does the day before the trash man makes his rounds. On one stoop, a large woman used a flyswatter to swat at a fly and then she swatted her son in response to something he said as he ran down the steps toward the street. Almost all these people had one thing in common: they paid no attention to Jody as he and Michael walked past.

The laundromat was a sauna. Its inside air was a dense bouquet of fabric softener and off-brand powder detergent and mildew and body odor. Except for a homeless man zigzagging the sidewalk outside, Jody was the only white person in sight. Nobody said a word, they just washed and dried and folded their clothes and kept to themselves, alone in the most populous city in the country. An elaborate composition of sounds reverberated among the silence: the repetitive metal-on-metal clanging of zippers and metal buttons tumbling in dryers on opposite sides of the establishment; the clumps of wet cotton spinning in the hot air inside the dryers; the dampened echo of quarters being fed into various machines one at a time; the buzzers announcing the completion of drying cycles; the sighs from people folding clothes at standing tables positioned at various intervals next to the change machines at the nucleus of the intramural space. The clamor of nothingness seemed to overwhelm the silence. The noise of cleaning, the sounds of removing the dirt and the stains from what would only become dirty and stained again, a futile desire to divest one's self of something that would never depart.

They perspired profusely in the damp, fragranced air, folding Michael's clothes next to a massive wheezing woman while waiting for some other clothes to dry when Michael's friend Wes appeared out of nowhere, materializing behind them without a sound. It was an unconventional spot to schedule a meeting, but then again Michael wasn't exactly conventional. Wes was a short, clean-cut black man in his late twenties or early thirties with fresh shoulder-length braids and trendy-without-being-too-trendy clothes: slim-but-not-too-skinny jeans, clean-but-not-too-flashy high-top sneakers, a red teeshirt with a small logo of some company Jody had never heard of, a pristine tan-leather messenger bag. He was clearly not from around here; somehow he fit in even less than Jody.

Jody begrudgingly helped Michael finish folding his last load into organized sorted-by-color piles and then Michael took these neatly separated stacks of cotton and crammed them back into the dank laundry bag in no discernible order. Jody witnessed a tear of sweat fall from his own nose onto the concrete floor. He wiped his forehead with his teeshirt's sleeve. The room felt like sitting in a steam bath without the promise of refreshment or cleansing. He noticed that Wes wasn't sweating at all, somehow defying all basic principles of human anatomy; he stayed dry their entire time at the laundromat, not even a droplet of sweat surfaced.

Wes spoke in good intentions as he passionately relayed his backstory to Jody. He worked for a small record label called Tommy Boy Records, which was affiliated with a subdivision of a subdivision of Warner Brothers, meaning he was somewhat "connected" in the music industry. Wes also managed a few musicians on the side, and Michael was one of those musicians. During their walk to the laundromat, Michael had told Jody about the development deal Wes had secured for him with Tommy Boy and how the record label was trying to branch out from its current hip-hop roster, hedging its bets with a few young talented singer-songwriters whose genre was sure to be the next big movement in popular music. Plus, Tommy Boy liked the novelty of signing a black singer-songwriter. Jody knew about development deals and knew he was lucky to have avoided one when he signed his first record contract at twenty-two—a lifetime ago now, everything seemed different these days, and twenty-two was worlds away. Jody knew that a development deal basically meant that Tommy Boy would front the money necessary to record an album for Michael, which was easy for an established record company to do because they already owned or had cheap access to a studio and they contracted a few engineers and second rate producers and had all the means to record a decent first album for a musician, all of which was great for the artist because it meant you didn't need to spend the five to twenty grand it took to record an album on your own. And better yet, if the label liked what you recorded, then they would sign you to a record contract. So it sounded like a win-win. But if the label was uncertain about your project, or if it simply didn't fit their current repertoire, then they wouldn't sign you, which seemed OK too because at least you got to record an album for free and now you could use the resulting recording to shop around to other labels who might be interested. The only catch was that if you found another record company who liked your music and wanted to offer you a record deal, the original company had first right of refusal (usually for two years or so), which meant they could then sign you after turning you down initially, often at a lesser percentage because they didn't have to bid against anyone. A lot of companies did this if a bigger label wanted to sign you (say, if Sony was suddenly interested, then you must be worth signing, but not until then; until then you would wait in patient obscurity among all the other chumps with development deals). This last part was the part of the deal that often hurt the artists, removing any negotiating power or leverage they might've had.

Michael was excited though, so Jody masked his skepticism behind a congratulatory smile and a literal pat on the back. After all, it was better than nothing. Wes told Jody he was going to help Michael record his solo album and shop it around for a record deal on an indie label if Tommy Boy didn't want it. Jody thought this was a good idea: if the big label didn't want it, go independent and you're less likely to get cock-blocked by the industry suits. Wes's sensibility made Jody like him even more.

While the trio hiked back to the apartment, Michael recollected a couple of his favorite stories from their tour for Wes, who commented on Jody's "flowing blond hair" on his second album.

"I thought you had maybe died or something," Wes said sarcastically. "You were the next big thing after that big single."

"Nope—still alive. Haven't played in a few years, but still alive." Jody replied. It felt good to have someone acknowledge that he once existed, though he brushed it off under a cloak of confidence.

Back at the apartment Jody toweled off and changed into a fresh teeshirt. Michael showered and dressed and then rehearsed the setlist for his show, which was only two nights away—Friday night in Manhattan. A solo acoustic set. It was his first time opening by himself for a national act—an alternative-rock group called The Spill Canvas. Wes had procured the gig for Michael a few weeks earlier and said he was working on a few other "big name" spots as well and mentioned those few "big names" with whom Jody was utterly unfamiliar. He understood how fly-by-night the industry could be and how four years ago *he* might have been one of the "big name" headlining acts for whom everyone wanted to open.

Wes and Jody occupied the dusty black futon while Michael played his set from a foldout metal chair that buckled slightly under his weight. Jody fingered a cigarette-burn hole on the futon's cloth surface while Michael fingerpicked his guitar. Wes typed the seven-song setlist into his iPhone as Michael practiced each song. *Everybody here has an iPhone*, Jody thought. He was an outsider, a tourist, an *i* without a *Phone*. Jody's teeshirt clung to his body, wicking the moisture. *Nobody here has air conditioning. All iPhones but no A/C.* Wes made a few recommendations on the song order, offered to buy Jody lunch tomorrow before Michael's show to "pick your brain about the music business," and before the sun set he disappeared from their day as quickly as he had appeared.

As daylight bid them goodbye, a handful of Michael's friends—a diversity poster of black and white and Hispanic twenty-somethings—arrived unannounced, coming and going without knocking. They used the restroom without asking and on more than one occasion opened the refrigerator door to reveal an upside-down empty ketchup bottle and a pickle jar containing urine-colored liquid and nothing else, all of which appeared to be regular occurrences. Michael paid them little attention and practiced his set into the twilight. As they came and went, Michael introduced these wayfarers one by one to Jody, each time referring to him as "my famous rockstar friend from back in Ohio," which pissed Jody off a little. Had it been anyone else he would have thought Michael was being disingenuous or even antagonistic, but instead he knew it was simply Michael's strange way of showing affection.

Michael and three of his friends left the apartment shortly after midnight. They invited Jody to travel with them on their latenight adventures, but he declined, citing a long day and jet lag and a need for sleep. He knew Michael wouldn't be back until 4 a.m. or later and he really did need some rest.

Just after midnight he had the apartment to himself. Futon. Three ashtrays brimming with butts. Two foldout chairs. The cluttered remains of the mysterious missing roommate. Several cockroach carcasses. A large fan propped in the window, blowing the midnight air into the apartment. Having smoked his last few cigarettes, he searched his duffle for his backup pack, rummaging through teeshirts and underwear, and when he found the pack it was crushed—a dust of tobacco fell from the cardboard container like ash. Not a single salvageable cigarette. *Fuck.* He searched the livingroom and then Michael's bedroom for just one nighttime cigarette (half of which he planned to smoke now and then save half for the morning), but he came up short on both accounts. Empty-handed. Nothing. And so he was faced with two choices: try to go to sleep without one (which meant he would have to face the morning without one as well), or find a twenty-four-hour store somewhere in Brooklyn. He chose the latter without much contemplation. He was tired but his authoritarian craving ran the show. So he slipped his boots on, grabbed the key Michael had left for him, coiled it onto his keychain so he wouldn't lose it, and hit the midnight streets of Bed-Stuy.

The night was unexpectedly calm—that thin sliver of time between the chaos of the day and the chaos of the night. His fifteen-block walk to Broadway was uneventful and eventually he found a King Qwik—a convenient store in which a man sat behind a necessarily redundant shield of metal bars and two-inch thick bulletproof glass and didn't say a word to Jody when he approached, displaying only a bothered look: *What do you want?*

"Two Marlboro Reds. Hard packs."

"Twenty-two," the man said, quoting the price with a thick Indian accent, rounding up, not attempting to calculate the tax. *Twenty-two dollars for some goddamn cigarettes.* He slid the money through the slot in the glass and the man reciprocated with two packs of Marlboros. Jody pocketed the cigarettes and footed it back to Putnam Ave. It was after 1 a.m. now and the midnight calm was fading. He heard thunder and then felt a droplet of rain. A storm was coming.

Jody walked the fifteen rain-soaked blocks back to the apartment. When he arrived, he climbed the porch steps slowly but with intent. Standing in the midnight rain in Bed-Stuy, he suddenly felt the weight of his life thrust upon him, so much so that he was certain he left bootprints in the concrete during his ascent.

When he was a boy, Jody's mother told him the story of Moses' ascent to the top of a mountain. She told him that God had commanded Moses to climb to the top, and when he got there, He commanded Moses to *be on the mountain.* She went on with the story, most of which Jody had forgotten years ago, but he always remembered being perplexed, even as a small boy, by the seeming redundancy of the story: why would God tell Moses to travel to the top of the mountain and then tell him to be on the mountain when he would obviously already *be on the mountain* after climbing such a great height? But Jody saw it differently now, as if it was a new story altogether. God was telling Moses to do a lot of hard work—to endure a lot of difficult shit—to get to the top of the mountain, and when Moses got there God didn't want him to start planning his descent or think about his past mistakes or worry about his past-due electric bill. He simply wanted Moses to take the time to appreciate the moment, to live in the moment, to *be on the mountain,* to just *be.*

The inside of Michael's apartment felt strangely like home to Jody. A new life in the moment. The gift of a new life ahead of him. No more past. Only now.

One of Michael's roommates had returned while Jody was gone. He was in his room with the door closed, already asleep. Jody could hear the droning of a small window A/C unit beyond the door to the sleeping roommate's bedroom. Jody lay on the livingroom's futon and yearned for a fraction of the relief that the air in the roommate's room could provide, and yet in many ways he knew that the relief he felt at this moment—the relief of a new life, one without a past—was far greater than any temporary relief that a change in temperature could bring. It was the momentary relief of immortality, a feeling of being alive.

He remained on the futon with his eyes open for a few minutes, tired but unable to fall asleep. He searched for sleep, but couldn't find it. Stand up, stretch. A glass of water from the sink. An Ambien from his duffle bag. The rain outside dissipated.

He counted gunshots in the distance, a taste of the real world outside the window, far enough away that he didn't feel unsafe, but close enough to remind him where he was and how different and cruel this world could be, and yet there was a magnificent beauty in this cruelty. The shots sounded like store-bought fireworks far off in the distance, a violent celebration. He listened and counted the pops of the small-bore firearm. Seventeen, eighteen, nineteen. Another sleeping pill. He stopped counting at forty-four.

Thoughts of Jolene and of the unborn baby, of his ex-wife, of Shelly from the bus, of how pointless this life might be without a past and how miserable it was with one. Thoughts are always the strangest at the nadir of the day, but even more so on a day like this, on a day when life felt like it had either no meaning or a totally new meaning, teetering on the brink of two extremes. But what was the meaning if there was one?

The storm outside had passed, but he couldn't quiet his own mind. He was trapped inside his head, inside his own private storm. He lay alone, with nothing to look back upon, searching for something to look forward to, something with meaning, any kind of meaning. The double dose of Ambien began to take hold.

Do we live just to die? Is self-gratification the only reason we were put here—to pursue our own self-interests? If not, then why is this our impulse? And why does this impulse always seem to lead to suffering? Why do we seek pleasure before anything else? Why do we avoid pain when it can lead to immense pleasure?

With the Ambien in his bloodstream, he hoped to avoid dreaming that night because his nights were too often filled with nightmares about his mother's death less than a year earlier. Plus he knew the Ambien could do strange things to his dreams, making them surreal, and yet somehow *more* real, extra real— more urgent, more panicked, more terrifying. By quarter till four, the sounds of the street through the screened window evanesced, as did reality in a moment of haze, the moment when the real world meets the dream world and both worlds coexist, if just for a moment, as though he could pull something out of the dreamworld and drag it back into reality if he were so inclined. He welcomed the sleep through the haze, embracing it like a catch-and-release fish being placed back into its pond, freeing it from everything terrible, and allowing it to roam the calm waters once more, free from danger, until it was caught again.

The dreamworld did not bring those nightmares about his mother. Instead, while his physical body was sprawled out and sweating on the futon, he saw Shelly dressed in the same white summer dress she had worn on the bus, her long, dark hair draped over her left shoulder. She stood in front of the evening sun in what appeared to be a field engulfed by fog somewhere inside the city, with shards of light beaming around her silhouette, the sun's rays fractured by a dense brume, obscuring everything in the distance. She was situated about fifteen feet from Jody. He attempted to speak but couldn't understand his own words as they left his mouth. She listened acutely as he spoke his babble. Word after word tumbled out in an indiscernible order, each word indecipherable from the one before. He had no idea what he was trying to communicate. He noticed only the incoherentness and complexity of everything he was trying to say. And when he finished his string of jumbled words, all of it drivel, she replied, "Simplicity is the essence of happiness," and smiled her same smile from the bus. Confused, Jody said, "What?" and she responded with only one sentence: "You can't get around what you have to go through." And then she pivoted and regressed in the direction of the light. The sunbeams flowed over her bare shoulders and between her bare legs, casting shadows on everything behind her. He gazed at her contemplatively. She represented everything beautiful about life. And now she was leaving him. Or perhaps she was saving him. He wasn't sure which.

When he woke the next morning, the sun shone through the livingroom's curtainless window directly onto his face. The room felt like the brightest place on earth. He sat up and tried to rub the headache from his head. Even the walls squinted from the sun. He stood in his underwear and placed his sunglasses on his face. The sun's rays followed his rise from the futon. The rest of the apartment was still. It smelled faintly of stale cigarettes and sweat. He looked at the blinking clock on the other side of the room and wondered what time it was. Adjusting his underwear, he noticed his erection. Thinking solely of himself and his headache and his most primal of needs, he remembered the dream. He needed coffee and a cigarette. And her. These were the only things that could bring him relief.

He pulled on a teeshirt, lit a cigarette, found the piece of paper with Shelly's number on it, and dialed the ten digits, hoping he could see her later that day. The phone rang and he waited to hear her tender voice. After two-and-a-half rings a tone overtook the speaker: "We're sorry, the number you have reached has been disconnected." *What?* He looked at the number again and compared it to the number he had just dialed.

She gave me the wrong fucking number? He set the phone on the windowsill and looked out the window, searching for the peace that came only with silence—the serenity of solitude. The reason the Catholic churches of his childhood had felt so peaceful was their utter quiet, a God-given gift of silence, the sound of absolute truth. Outside, a flock of unseen birds chirped louder than they should be allowed to chirp. Jody massaged the headache from his temples and peeked out at the world through squinted eyes. A child played with a basketball in the street. Something out of sight scared the birds and they scattered beautifully, making everything right in the world, if just for a moment. With the birds out of earshot, everything in Brooklyn was quiet. At peace. He could almost hear himself think. Goodmorning. The sun set fire to the sky.

SERIAL KILLERS

New York Times
January 31, 2006
Review by Samantha Nelson
★★☆☆☆ 2/5 Stars

It appears that Ohio-based singer-songwriter Jody Grafton attempted to convey a single message with his second major-label release, *Out of the Storm*. And that message is that the American alt-rock band The Killers could make a good acoustic album. Although he has a limited vocal range, it's not like Grafton can't sing; he simply sings much too much like The Killers' familiar frontman, Brandon Flowers — so much so that *Out of the Storm* could plausibly pass as The Killers' first acoustic album to casual listeners.

While the songwriting shines through on songs like the title track and "I Won't Be There When You're Alone," Grafton's tone and cadence are far too similar to Flowers' to be taken seriously. Like Flowers, Grafton's scratchy vocals are sprawled-out behind the microphone, his words a mixture of monotone song and lackadaisical speech, his tales of sorrow plentiful.

The surprising success of *Out of the Storm* was a slow burn; it didn't catch mainstream attention until the album's third single, "Ohio Again," torched dozens of college radio stations throughout the U.S., turning the spark into a scorching wildfire overnight, leading Grafton to Top 40 success on mainstream radio and a 69-city, international headlining tour.

Although the album lacks diversity, it does have some promising moments. On the album's best track, "Rain Without Lightning," Grafton bellows about a deep loneliness: "Now there's no one to talk to / nowhere to think." And the anti-love love song, "Before It's Over Again," does a solid job of conveying that between-relationships feeling we've all felt: "Looking over your shoulder / said you'd never run away / But now your feet are moving / doesn't being alone make you afraid?" By the end of *Out of the Storm*'s final track — the aforementioned, piano-riddled single, "Ohio Again" — the album seems to fulfill what it set out to accomplish, leaving listeners hungry for a Brandon Flowers's acoustic album.

FALLING WHILE SITTING DOWN

As an adult now, the Boy felt removed from his youth, a childhood that had subsided at the ragged edges of humanity, but he didn't entirely realize his childhood's desultory nature until much later, when he had fully grown and matured and experienced a different kind of life, a life in which the world seemed less chaotic and less turbid but also perhaps less real, at least in the sense that his old world seemed more authentic and less affected than the new "adult" world he had discovered once he was out on his own, a world of money and power and emotions he could not convey with words, not even much later when the Boy approached thirty and was no longer a Boy at all and had long ago left home and discovered the world for himself, eventually realizing the new world was just as cruel and confusing as the one he had left behind more than a decade earlier.

The Boy was brought into this world at the tail-end of Generation X, a solipsistic and self-centered Me Generation, a disaffected and directionless generation, a generation the Boy both rejected and identified with, which was confusing for him later in life. He had been an accidental birth, born to a forty-two-year-old bipolar Father and a thirty-six-year-old alcoholic Mother—a dysfunctional family before *dysfunctional* was popular. Besides debilitating manic-depression, the Boy's Father —whose IQ significantly exceeded 140—suffered from schizophrenia and had persistent, elaborate relationships with people who did not exist in the physical world, people who conspired to ruin his life. The Boy's first memory was of the Father extinguishing a cigarette on the Mother's bare chest just below her clavicle while she struggled to get away. The Boy still had nightmares about it twenty-five years later, even after multiple sessions with two highly regarded psychotherapists. The Boy was three when the Mother left the Father; she started drinking more heavily around the same time. The Mother was a devout Catholic. The Father was broad-shouldered with a swimmer's musculature, silver-haired, and people often compared him to a well-known movie star of his era. He was taller than most tall men, and large in an ex-football-player kind of way—three times the size of the Mother, who was prettier than he was handsome. Together they were two wasted bodies of flesh in their torment. After the Mother and the Boy left the Father, the Boy saw him only one other time, at Christmas, when he was seven. The Father died of a heart attack when the Boy was nine. Years later he found the Father's death certificate; it noted advanced-stage alcoholic cardiomyopathy as the cause of the heart failure. The Boy's only memory of the Father's funeral was of the Mother struggling with a broken umbrella at the burial ceremony underneath a pessimistic under-illuminated sky, the top spring failing to hold the umbrella's runner in place, causing the umbrella to collapse in on itself. The Father left them to some of their loneliest nights. The Boy did not remember the six-hour drive to the funeral. Nor did he remember the return trip. The downpour at the gravesite was torrential and unforgiving.

For much of the Boy's preadolescent years he thought money came in two colors: green and white. The Mother sometimes sold their white bills at a 2:1 ratio—fifty cents on the dollar—because she could purchase alcohol with only the green bills. The Boy never saw any of the government-mandated nutritional pamphlets that were delivered with the white bills at the beginning of each month. The Mother earned minimum wage whenever she was able to work full-time, but she was unable to hold a job for any appreciable period of time because when she drank she went on benders in which she stayed shut-in in their one-bedroom duplex apartment for days at a time, often not eating while drinking heavily and chain smoking Salem Lights from a green soft pack, stumbling and falling down and ensconcing herself on the ash-daubed couch, somehow defying the laws of physics by falling while sitting down. When she was drinking she avoided contact with the physical world. The vast majority of her caloric intake during these benders was alcoholic. Red wine was the Mother's preferred drink, though she settled for tall cans of Milwaukee's Best—or whatever beer was least expensive that week—when she could not afford the bottom-shelf wines at the liquor store seven tedious blocks from their apartment. Those blocks were most difficult on the Mother's return trip from the liquor store. The walk *to* the store was always fueled with buzz-filled exhilaration and anticipation, both of which placed a heavy fog over her shame, but the walk back was comprised of a nervous expectancy, much like a child returning from the local supermarket with a newly purchased toy, usually removing the plastic thing's complicated packaging and playing with the toy in the car before making it halfway home. Similarly, the Mother couldn't wait to unpackage her brown paper bag on the way home—*I'll just have one beer*—and so the last three blocks were the hardest part of her trek home, at times resulting in her halting to rest on one of several benches, all of which were public benches, except for one swinging bench nestled on a private porch, and if she stopped to rest she almost assuredly had another beer—*just one more just to take the edge off* —and on numerous occasions someone would find the ninety-pound woman drunk and asleep on a bench just a few blocks from her home, brown paper bag in her clutch. The Mother had been arrested twice. The liquor store's owner sometimes allowed her to purchase beer or wine on store credit. The Mother would return to their cockroach-infested apartment, which stank of urine and empty beer cans and stale cigarette smoke, and when she was too drunk to venture into the kitchen to find the trashcan, the Mother's *modus operandi* was to hide her empty beer cans under the front flap at the base of the couch. Sometimes she was unable to make it to the bathroom on her own. The couch cushions had been flipped dozens of times. The roaches appeared to come from the next-door Neighbor's apartment. The Neighbor was a kind and lonely man, a WWII veteran in his mid-seventies who seemed to own three or four apartments worth of possessions and who didn't mind the bugs, perhaps because he had seen far worse, or maybe because they kept him company. The Neighbor ate fried-egg sandwiches and never cleaned the greasy skillet on the stovetop, the Boy remembered. *Love thy neighbor* was the Matthew 22 scripture the Mother muttered to herself every time she killed a cockroach with her house slipper, but when she drank, the scripture often morphed into *Fuck thy Neighbor* and throughout most of the Boy's childhood he thought they were two different biblical passages, a sort of Old Testament vs. New Testament contradiction. The Boy wondered why the electricity in their apartment went out far more frequently than at the Neighbor's apartment. And when it went out in winter, and it was too cold to stay inside, the Mother and the Boy had special "sleepovers" at various men's houses, one of whom was a large Man who wore a tie, which the Boy thought of as unusual because none of the men who lived in the Boy's neighborhood wore ties other than on Sundays. This neck-tied Man was years later convicted of several counts of child molestation. The Boy did not want to remember much about that Man, so he didn't. The Mother regularly slept the afternoons away while the Boy played G.I. Joe with his meager collection of action figures, carefully placing each figure back into plastic bins in an organized and methodical way when he was done, systematically separating the good guys into one bin and the bad guys into another bin and their weapons into yet a third bin (and every so often a few of the men switched sides from bad to good and vice versa). Grocery bags would sometimes materialize at the apartment's doorstep next to the gap where three missing wooden planks used to be on their deteriorating porch. The Mother told the Boy that she had prayed to St. Anthony and that he had found them some food. There were extended periods of time when the Boy subsisted on St. Anthony's peanutbutter and white bread and packaged sugary foods such as Pop-Tarts and Fruit Roll-Ups.

The Boy was what his teachers referred to as a "latchkey kid," walking home from school as early as age six to an empty house while the Mother worked a second-shift job, or coming home and opening the door and finding the Mother passed out on the couch, a cigarette still burning in the ashtray, an inch-and-a-half of undisturbed ash burned down to the filter. At school the Boy made friends with various elements of certain fringe social blocs—the nerds, the loners, the skaters, &c.—although he never attempted to adapt to their tenets or fully integrate into any one particular group, except that by age twelve the Boy almost exclusively kept company with the minorities of Midville Junior High, most notably the black children in his same grade, as well as a small number of Hispanic children, of whom there were no more than a few. It was the first time in his life that the Boy felt accepted by a particular group of people. The town's black population, which constituted roughly fifteen percent of the town's total population, lived almost exclusively in the same neighborhood as the Boy, making his affiliation to the group more logical geographically, and over a period of time he conformed to their customs, mannerisms, and cultural idiosyncrasies, like their baggy clothes, their close-cut hair, their rap music, and the distinctive phonetic changes in their vernacular, such as the lack of dental fricatives (e.g., "dis" in place of "this" and "munt" rather than "month"), the realization of final -ng sounds in function morphemes and content morphemes with two syllables (e.g., "trippin" in lieu of "tripping" and "runnin" as opposed to "running"), the reduction in final consonant clusters (e.g., "tes" instead of "test" and "han" in preference to "hand"), the reduction of certain diphthong forms to monophthongs (e.g., "boil" was pronounced as "ball" by several of the Boy's friends), the use of metathesised words (e.g., "aks" as an alternative to "ask" and "graps" as a substitute for "grasp"), and the unique stress placement in certain multisyllabic words like "police," "guitar," and "Detroit," which were pronounced by the Boy with initial stress instead of ultimate stress so those words sounded more like PO-leece, GAH-tar, and DEE-troit, respectively.

Before the Boy was a teenager, his Best Friend—a black child from the neighborhood—moved in with the Boy and the Mother. The Mother didn't notice for several weeks that the Best Friend had been living at their apartment. The Best Friend's Father still had the better part of a fifteen-year prison stint to serve for armed robbery and his (biological) Mother was addicted to crack cocaine and was somehow worse off than the Boy's own Mother. The Boy and the Best Friend became inseparable by age twelve and the town's people rarely saw one without the other. The Boy and the Best Friend became brothers, closer in fact than most siblings who shared the same genes. They shared a small futon mattress on the Boy's bedroom floor. By age thirteen the Boy was the tallest kid in his grade. The Mother said he looked a great deal like the Father, especially in his face, and the Boy secretly thought the Mother hated him for it, and in truth the Mother did hate how the Boy reminded her of the Father and of the Father's torment, which still haunted her a decade after she took the Boy and ran, but she did not hate the Boy for it; she thought of it as only an unfortunate reminder that she could not escape her past. By age fourteen the Boy was fully integrated with his new group of friends, carrying all the responsibilities of an adult at this point. He had a dishwashing job outside of school and he and the Best Friend returned home whenever they chose to return home, unconcerned with a curfew. On his sixteenth birthday, the Mother gave the Boy her sobriety and an acoustic guitar, the latter of which came from a pawn shop on the other side of town. The Boy was uncertain where the sobriety came from. At first he thought of it as one of the periods in which the Mother would stop drinking for an extended period of time—she had many times stopped drinking for several consecutive months in the past—and then the Boy thought he would eventually return home late one night and find her once again off the wagon, but this time was different, this time the Mother kept her seat on the wagon. It was unclear to the Boy what triggered this newfound vigor for a life of temperance, and it was hard to swallow after watching the Mother struggle for so many years, and yet every night when the Boy returned home he cringed when he opened the door, tentatively placing the key in the lock, fully expecting to see the Mother sprawled out on the couch, semi-conscious with an inch-and-a-half of ash dangling from the tip of a burning cigarette in the ashtray, but every time he came home she was awake and friendly and productive, an abstemious new woman, and within a few months the Mother found a better-than-minimum-wage job at a local attorney's office, and so she and the Boy and the Best Friend moved to a slightly nicer apartment without cockroaches in a cul-de-sac neighborhood on the other side of town, and the Mother cooked hearty meals for the Boy and the Best Friend several times a week, and yet every day when he opened the door the feeling never changed, and not knowing whether she was going to return to drinking again was in many ways worse than coming home to her drunk and passed out. It was a different kind of hell knowing that any day she could relapse, because that was all the Boy knew, that was what she was supposed to do, that was what was normal. The Boy moved out of the Mother's home the day he turned eighteen, toting a guitar case and a duffle bag and a bunch of future regrets.

RETURN OF THE SONGWRITER

SPIN Magazine
February 27, 2006
Interview by Kent Everly

Jody Grafton isn't what we've come to expect from the belly of the modern music industry. He isn't a faux-rocker or a wannabe-superstar or an attention-grabbing new musician. Rather, he is a real songwriter: a prodigious young man who writes brilliant, expressive lyrics over sparse acoustic instrumentals.

Last year, Grafton released his second album, *Out of the Storm*, which experienced lukewarm sales until the single "Ohio Again" was picked up by radio stations across the country. At age 24, Grafton conjures the experiences of an older, more mature man, a man who has lived through a lifetime of poor decisions and now wallows in his own regrets and discontent.

I met Grafton in Williamsburg, Brooklyn while he was in New York for a live performance. He was not late for our meeting, which informs us of Jody Grafton the man more than you might understand. Unlike many musicians I've interviewed, he didn't need to postpone or reschedule our meeting, nor did he make me wait to talk to him. In fact, he beat me to the diner where we rendezvoused.

I recognized him almost immediately. He looked like he had dwelled in Brooklyn for the last decade, not some Midwestern Rustbelt city: sunglasses, tattoos, a thick mane of James Dean hair, and a solemn look on his face. When I arrived he was doing nothing but looking out the window, observing the moment. He wasn't texting or talking on a cellphone, he wasn't preoccupied with the day's events, he wasn't hurried to get finished with the interview — he was present. I talked and he listened. I asked questions and he pondered and responded with words that felt like truth.

We talked about his first album, *Into the Storm*, which few people had heard in the mainstream until recently. We talked about his latest record and why it took six months for it to pick up steam and get noticed by the radio. We contrasted the two albums and we both agreed on their differences: where his vocals mingled with the acoustic guitar on his first album, his gravelly voice and troubles-of-the-past lyrics disciplined the sparse instrumentation on his new release. "The albums weren't considerably different," Grafton admits. "I had written half the new record right after the first one, so I was pretty much in the same state of mind — just the sound matured a bit."

Grafton has matured rapidly as well. He is an intelligent, articulate young man. His manner is relaxed and cordial, yet street-wise. His deep speaking tone is at odds with his gruff, world-weary singing voice, which carries with it a hint of rugged beauty. His songs seem to come from the ends of dusty roads and endless nights that keep on stretching, feeling as if they'll never turn.

When asked about how he developed his singing

style, he treads lightly. "I've been on the road a lot, and as you go along you pick up all these things you hear out in the world, you know? The process of learning how to use your own voice is a reductive thing. You strip down those influences until what's left is, more or less, essentially what you do. You just drive until you get wherever you're going. And you end up singing how you sing, and writing how you write, without thinking much about how you got there."

When asked about his influences, Grafton says he listens to more hip-hop than rock or folk music. Listening to his music, you probably wouldn't guess that he's more influenced by Jay-Z than Bob Dylan. "It's basically like listening to recorded poetry, especially the stuff from the nineties — my teenage years. I don't know what it is, but something about that kind of music just resonates with me. It feels realer and more honest than most of what you hear on the radio these days."

Over the last two months his new record has received overwhelming praise from dozens of publications. But Grafton says he doesn't want to read the reviews anymore. "You can get addicted to that stuff, addicted to the praise. But you can also obsess over the bad stuff; even the tiniest criticism in the positive reviews can mess up your day." *Paste* magazine called his new album "brilliantly quiet" and "gritty, staggeringly beautiful," while *Rolling Stone* labeled Grafton a "gifted new songwriter." But he is haunted by cavils and incongruities.

"I read the *Rolling Stone* thing, and sure, I thought it was really, really nice to get four stars — I really did, it was great — but it felt like they were reviewing a Radiohead album or a Kanye West album or something. They certainly weren't describing my record. They said something like the songs felt hopeless and weren't redemptive. But for me, sure the album was about a shitty past and a shitty present, but it alluded to the potential for a good future on the horizon. Hell, maybe it didn't come off that way on the record, I don't know, but that's how I felt when I was writing it."

And it's the negative reviews that truly bring out the neurotic in Grafton. "I almost lost my breakfast when I read [the *New York Times*] bit." Last month, the *Times* compared him to Brandon Flowers, the monotone frontman for The Killers, claiming *Out of the Storm* lacked diversity and could "plausibly pass as The Killers' first acoustic album to casual listeners."

Out of the Storm is diverse in a narrow sense. It's true that the album comes across as dark and hopelessly depressed at times, but these are emotional states that most people can identify with. "I don't know why I find it interesting to wallow in that stuff," Grafton said. "And I don't think of the songs as one-dimensional; I think they're kind of well-rounded. I think there's darkness, sure, there's some gloomy stuff there, there's a lot of awkward sad moments, but I think there's a lot of humor in the songs, even if you're just pointing and laughing at me. And I feel like most of the songs, not all of them, but I would say most of my songs are optimistic or hopeful in some weird way, but they dig into anxiety, they dig into just sort of trying to figure out what it feels like to want somebody or to miss somebody or — I think most music is dealing with love or sex or friendships or fear or just celebrating being irresponsible or something — and I don't think my music is really any different than most. It's just maybe the way I package it or the way I deliver it that is sort of swelling in some sort of emotional way. I mean it's dark, but it's not Nirvana. Hopefully there's the right mixture of hope and despair."

Perhaps what people see as overly dark is just Grafton's version of the truth. He specializes in lyrics that cut right through listeners with their sincerity and honesty. With a tender, scratchy voice that sometimes cracks with emotion, and a clear understanding of the vivid storytelling that defines folk music, he commands attention effortlessly. This young songwriter already has the wisdom to know that if you're going to serve up a blood-drenched hate-ballad, you best have an old soul's voice to sing it with. Every line rings with desperation and a desire for salvation.

Notwithstanding his Brooklyn bohemian appearance, one listen to his new album reveals Grafton as a young Midwesterner who writes hard-bitten songs of family tragedies and sings them in a voice that's as sun-bleached and wind-battered as an Ohio cornfield. Although the sound is different from a traditional folk record, the enigmatic lyrics are wrapped in familiar Americana. The instrumentation is meticulous, nothing sounds out of place, especially the aching violins, which are used with remarkable restraint. *Out of the Storm* is convincing from its opening line, "I traveled here with a bag of regrets," through its solemn last words: "I'm done with this life."

PART TWO || Lost Songs

BEYOND THE BOTTOM OF A GLASS

The days after the crash were the hardest. The Troubled Man sat by himself on a creaking, off-kilter barstool and ordered another round, lit another cigarette, and searched for meaning amongst the wreckage, hunting for some nameless thing under the gray tavern lights, losing count of his whiskey-and-waters, inspecting the bottom of each glass. He couldn't find meaning there, so he kept searching.

Taverns such as this one carried a desolation that swept aside words and dull sentiment. The Troubled Man asked the barkeep for another round—a shot and a pint. He coiled his fingers through the mug's handle; his eyes weren't his own when he peered down at the liquid inside. The mug was filled with hope. He closed his eyes and brought it to his ready lips. It tasted like truth. He detached the glass from his mouth and returned it to the blurry bar top. It felt too cold to touch.

When it was time to leave, the Troubled Man paid the bartender, squinting at the mystery of his crumpled money. He had a difficult time delivering his head out beyond the tavern doors. The world outside seemed even darker. A homeless man, alone in the middle of the street, pushed a ragged-wheeled shopping cart. A lonely bumpersticker on the empty cart read, *Ohio is alright if you've never been anywhere else.*

DAYS AFTER THE CRASH

Jody Grafton was not an illusionist, but he was good at making things disappear. He could not, however, disappear the morning. Today's buckshot morning was unavoidable. He squinted in agony as the sun's rays spotlighted the nicotine-bruised walls that swallowed Michael's pathetic apartment. Vague reminders of last night were scattered around him. Dirty clothes. Fast-food wrappers. Empty beer cans.

He made his way up the fire escape to the roof one story above the apartment, balancing his guitar and a black coffee. From the rooftop he worked his lighter until the first cigarette of the day was lit. Tattooed arms protruded from his teeshirt's sleeves, skin inked with the scars of a past life. His right forearm displayed FUTURE REGRETS in faded blue ink, ornamented by sparse musical notes and colorful embellishments that didn't add up to much more than what they were—garish filler, not unlike much of his twenties. His old world had ended over the last year, and yet he wasn't yet accustomed to this new world.

Here he was, a year from thirty, already facing the wreckage of his self-indulgent twenties.

A New York sunburn summer had overtaken the borough: azure blue sky to the west, early morning sun to the east, the complete sum of endless blue heavens scattered above him, juxtaposed with storm clouds in the northern distance, the paradoxical promise of sunshine and rain. Near the open area's only door, dead center of an otherwise empty rooftop, Jody sat beneath the shade of a three-foot awning—the only shelter from Mother Nature's temper. He sat on a tarnished metal chair that thousands of asses had christened over the years and tuned his Gibson by ear. Breathing the dense Bed-Stuy Brooklyn air, he searched the ether for a song, thinking into the blankness of the morning.

The sounds of the neighborhood seemed oddly layered this morning—the silvery symmetry of nature offset by man's dominion over it. Birds chirping. An elevated train in the distance. A gust of wind rustling a nearby tree. A fan in the window of some unseen apartment below. The distinct absence of cars and people and gunfire. He felt calm now as he picked and strummed, searching his chords and his words for euphony. The air felt drier on his skin today, as if the stainless-steel sky had sucked up the earth's humidity, preparing the vapors for something more sinister.

Jody sipped his coffee as storm clouds closed in on Brooklyn. He had two speeds when writing songs: lethargic and breakneck, the latter of which rarely happened and seemed to occur only during life's extremes, and yet Jody felt both today: he felt the amphetaminic rush of a new life, the potential for a fresh start, thankful for the gift of everything around him; but he also could not shake the sedative weight of the past, the feeling of loss and sorrow and mourning, the reminder of so many mistakes, of so many things left undone, and so with his guitar he explored the peaks and valleys of his life, attempting to chisel a song from the stones of both extremes.

Jody heard thunder in the distance. The rain came and baptized every surface on the rooftop and the awning above his head and the rest of the neighborhood around him, bringing forth the sounds of nature and of a different world, washing away the sins from the night before. The rainfall dampened the acoustics in the air, blessing his Gibson with a somber sound that he used to his advantage. It was an abnormal kind of rain, dark and cheerless and dreary throughout most of the Stygian sky, although Jody could also see sunlight beaming through a few gaping apertures among the clouds. Depending on his perspective, it was either raining on a sunny day or the sun was coruscating through the clouds on a rainy day, and it was up to *him* to decide which perspective was true, but he didn't want to be the one to decide; he didn't want it to be *his* choice, based on *his* perspective. He wanted it to be overwhelmingly sunny or depressingly overcast, but not both. But this was not within his control. And so it rained, and as it rained the sun's rays tickled the street below. He slipped on his Ray-Bans and picked at his guitar and drank his coffee, and after a while the amalgamation of sun and rain was not unlike the process of writing a song: there were the sunny days—not many of them, but they did exist—and on those days everything felt right and everything just worked and he felt exhilarated and euphoric and he couldn't stop thanking the sky for those days; and then there were the rainy days—of which there were more than enough—and those were the days in which nothing seemed to work and it was frustrating and bleak and it made him want to stop playing music and writing songs altogether; and then there was the rare occasion on which the sun and the rain converged and what he experienced was an entire continuum of emotions, from elation and lust to depression and anger and rage and almost everything in-between, love and hate at the same time, and those were the days he remembered most. It was the thrill of these extremes that kept him coming back for more.

And so he closed his eyes behind his dark sunglasses and listened to the rain and plucked the strings softly and found a melody from the emptiness between the sounds, finding beauty beneath the banality. Music was the one thing that allowed him to think without thinking at all. It required no cerebration on his part—movement of the hands without movement of the mind. The sounds and the words had the rare ability every so often to create a peak experience, one of those rare times when he literally trembled with excitement. This trembling reminded him that he was alive, right here on this rooftop in Brooklyn.

Brooklyn. He realized he hated this place, and yet he could stay here forever—a suitable punishment for the havoc he'd wreaked back in Ohio over the last decade. He was running from something—or someone—but he wasn't entirely sure what. Maybe it was his ex-wife—a wonderful woman for whom he was no longer the right person. Maybe it was his pregnant girlfriend —a miserable woman to whom he was now perpetually shackled. Maybe it was his one-hit-wonder musical career—a cocaine-high of short-lived stardom accompanied by his crash into oblivion. Maybe it was his mother's death last year—a traumatic event he hadn't yet reconciled. There had to be something for which he must repent. But things hadn't always been this way, and his life hadn't always been held together by trepidation and disdain and by the sum of what love wasn't.

At the height of his songwriting days he treated it like a blue-collar American-style day job, putting in long hours, often writing and practicing his craft for sixty hours a week, and when he played live gigs for obnoxiously small crowds in shithole after shithole, he was grateful to be able to do what he loved and treated those hole-in-the-wall bars like he was playing in front of a sold out Madison Square Garden, brimming night after night with over-capacity crowds, screaming fans chanting for one more encore, when in reality he never played an encore nor was he asked for one by the few dozen drunken sets of ears who tolerated his set over rounds of beers and lonely conversations and empty hearts, many of whom treated his performance like the sounds from an old jukebox, errant background music, the soundtrack to their sorrows, Jody's strumming and raspy voice and occasional Johnny Cash cover song accenting the taste of hops in their seventh or eighth beer, his musical recollection of sorrow mixed with shots of distilled malt and juniper berries to wash away their sorrows, and as he sang he did so with closed eyes, imagining the larger crowds in front of his future self, though stardom didn't happen overnight, he knew that's not how it usually happened, because you had to put in your time, had to pay your dues, and after a while the crowds of two dozen turned into three or four dozen and eventually approached triple digits, and as the crowds grew they became less intoxicated and more interested in his music, more interested in *him*, and more and more patrons honestly showed up to see *him* in Toledo and Grand Rapids and Saginaw and Muncie and dozens of other Midwestern towns, and his name rang out on old marquees and chalkboards placed on sidewalks in front of venues—TONIGHT: JODY GRAFTON $2 DRAFTS—and before he realized it he was earning enough money to pay for his food and gasoline and even a motel to sleep in instead of sleeping at another rest stop reclined in the driver's seat of his car and brushing his teeth and fixing his hair in the rest stop's sink and looking in the mirror and wondering whether any of this was ever going to pan out, because it was all panning out now and so he stopped worrying since he had his own sink and his own bed and some of the motels even had desks upon which he could spread out the lyrics to new songs, songs that hadn't yet been sung by him or by anyone, leaving the motel rooms to eat real meals at Denny's and Waffle House and small-town diners with forgettable names, not worrying whether he would have to walk out on the check because he didn't have enough to pay, and then one day, just before his twenty-second birthday, as the Midwest humidity captured the air, he looked up from three years of gigs and furious performances and he knew he had made it, he knew something had somehow changed, and those years of writing and performing had finally paid off, like a ballet dancer's daily practice would eventually allow her to move gracefully, elegantly, effortlessly on stage, no longer thinking, just doing, her muscles moving without her brain's commands, like Jody's fingers picking and his grating vocals crying out without thought of what chords to play or what lyrics to make melody, as if the universe knew when he was ready for his next step, as if the world was waiting for him to finish rehearsal behind the wooden doors of countless Midwestern taverns before the real show could begin, before he could move on to his true calling, and then when Jody took the stage for one last rehearsal in front of a crowd of nearly two-hundred on the outskirts of Indianapolis, he met a record executive named Joe Wheeler and that night was the pivotal night, the night when things changed, the night when the practice ended and the performance began.

And now it seemed as if the rays of light through the clouds over Brooklyn promised a brighter future, but the clouds themselves reminded Jody of the past. He thought of his mother, and for the first time since her death eight months earlier, he attempted to deal with her passing, to eulogize her on this rooftop, a thousand miles from home. He fingerpicked and hammered on the strings, finding the ideal chords, searching the eighth and sixteenth notes for the proper words to describe the time before her eternal rest. He sang slowly, deliberately, from the pit of his stomach and conjured up the lyrics to express his feelings:

It's been too long / for me to go back
To try to change / the demons of my past

Some songs are art, others are simply truth. Jody quickly scribbled a tentative title at the top of the page, looking at the name of the song and waiting for it to feel right, staring at the words as if they might slip off the page. As quickly as those lines removed themselves from his pen, a few more lines materialized out of his moist breaths:

I was unfair to you / and now you're gone
Every fading memory / of where things went wrong

These lines marked the beginning of a song steeped in melancholy. The words took him back to Ohio and the months leading up to his mother's death last September. As the rain fell around him he could feel her in the song. It's strange, people don't know how to love the ones they love until they disappear from their lives.

As a child Jody hardly knew his father, and so he found it impossible to respect the man. And his mother's rampant alcoholism, which began while he was in grade school, made it hard for him to connect with her as he grew older. Even though she stumbled into sobriety after Jody grew up and moved out of the house, it was impossible for him to forget the damage done during his youth. The bottle had captured his mother, hiding her away, making her physically present but strangely inaccessible, as if Jody had never experienced parenting at all, an orphan of sorts, forced to parent himself, to shoulder the responsibility of raising and protecting himself. As an adult it was harder for Jody to even think about his mother—her sobriety didn't draw him closer to her, and her past indiscretions haunted him.

Not knowing what to do with his life after teetering through high-school graduation, Jody found it hard to make a living. He'd moved out of the house as soon as he turned eighteen, and he didn't speak to his mother for more than a year. She wasn't even his one phone call when he was arrested a month after his nineteenth birthday.

After high school Jody moved from Midville with his best friend and his brother, Eric and Gray. Life's expenses were inexpensive. Rent, food, beer, and gasoline were their only necessities, so they acquired terrible, minimum-wage jobs to keep the vessel afloat, but none of them had much tolerance for authority, and within eight months the three of them had been collectively fired from eight different jobs, including four fast-food restaurants, two warehouses, one retail store, and a call center. By that spring, less than a year after high school, they were all three unemployed, and worse, they realized they were essentially unemployable.

With no job and no money Jody tried the next best thing: selling marijuana to college kids to make ends meet, an endeavor that lasted less than a year and ended as soon as Jody realized he didn't have the constitution for it, realizing firsthand what the outcome of that lifestyle would be: the inevitable end result—death or jail—was a cliche in every poor neighborhood in America.

So with barely enough money to eat, he and Eric started playing acoustic shows at local venues. Jody had latched onto music as a teen, and his obsession grew into his early twenties, and so teaming with his best friend to play songs together seemed like the right move. To keep his mind off everything—his lack of money, his childhood, his mother's ride on the wagon—Jody began honing his craft, playing guitar and writing god-awful songs every day, staying in his apartment for long stretches, hardening the calluses on his fingertips with hours of nonstop picking and strumming. It quickly became evident that Eric was not as serious about the craft, or perhaps Eric was simply less obsessed. A talented musician in his own right, Eric enjoyed playing shows with Jody, but Jody was in it for the long haul, and Eric wasn't prepared to dedicate that much of his life to anything. So Eric showed up occasionally, playing shows with his friend from time to time, but Jody stayed focused, and for a few years music was the most important thing in his life, often the *only* thing in his life—an escape from life itself.

During those years, Jody's mother, Irene, slowly crept back into his life. When Jody turned twenty-one, she was fifty-seven, a petite older woman, pretty in many of the ways older women are pretty, a tiny woman, more than a foot shorter than her son. It was easy to imagine how beautiful she must have been thirty years earlier, before the drinking, before the troubles, before Jody. Now, whenever Jody saw her, her "five years sober" keychain dangled proudly from her hand, though she still chain-smoked a pack a day and it showed in her blotchy skin and sepia teeth.

Irene's wrinkles had deepened by the time she reached sixty. Her leathery crevasses showcased years of hardship, although it felt like those years were behind her and these wrinkles were only a reminder of a stale past. She dedicated her early sixties to repairing her relationship with her son. Even though she never actually liked his music, she told herself that she just didn't understand it. She had both of his albums proudly on display in her kitchen next to framed posters of his album covers, and she bragged to her friends about her "famous son," her "son who is on tour at the moment," her "son who was featured in the *New York Times*." Her friends didn't understand his music either—they were more in tune with Gregorian chant than with Jody's acoustic-rock music—but they smiled when Irene told them about her son's success, congratulating her to her face, surreptitiously talking about Jody's excessive tattoos and unconventional occupation when they congregated after Sunday Mass.

Of the hundreds of shows Jody played during his early twenties, Irene attended exactly four. These were four shows to which her son had personally invited her. They were held in calmer venues with decent-sized crowds. He intentionally avoided bringing her to many of his early gigs for good reasons: he felt embarrassed at times to be playing in front of inattentive, drunken crowds; he didn't want her to suffer the temptation of the bars in which he played; and he knew she wasn't that interested in the music. Sure, she loved her son, and he loved her —a love birthed out of mutual understanding and mutual struggle—but they both knew, even though neither of them spoke about it, that she wasn't interested in the specifics of what he did. She was proud of her son's accomplishments, much like the mother of an astrophysicist, proud of the success but unconcerned with the details.

By twenty-seven, Jody had had enough of the music industry, enough of its politics, enough of its fly-by-night successes, enough of the musicians with no talent being promoted by inept suit-and-tie A&R guys who didn't know a thing about music. So, after the release of his third album, an under-promoted and commercially unsuccessful endeavor, he was dropped from his record label, and he stopped. He stopped making music, he stopped playing shows, he put his guitars away and didn't play at all. He didn't want to think about it any longer. For the longest time he didn't do anything except sit at home and drink and smoke Marlboros and dabble in various narcotics and disassociate from the outside world. For nearly two years, his life was bathed in sorrow, and he wasn't entirely sure why. He had accomplished everything he'd wanted to accomplish —everything he was *supposed* to accomplish—and yet he wasn't happy, he didn't feel fulfilled, he didn't feel as though his life mattered, and so he drank to dull the pain, and when that stopped working he drank even more and threw things around the house, and when that accomplished nothing he threw more stuff and broke things and argued with his (now former) wife, yelling and fighting over everything, yelling and fighting over nothing. Sometimes a man has to hit both walls before he can find the middle.

Desolation. Depression. Rock bottom. Is this what he'd been waiting for his entire life? His own life reminded him of a dying seagull, flying in ever-diminishing circles, defecating on everything in its descent. But before he hit the ground, he received a phone call from his mother. She left him a message, and even though her words didn't say it, her tone was outfitted in a fear that told of a return to the bottle, weighted down with loss and lost pride.

"Jody, it's yer mother. I needa taltah yah. Call me back when yah get this honey."

Buzzed from spirits and anger, his finger dialed the first six numbers and then hovered over the keypad. He closed his eyes and waited to dial the seventh. He thought that maybe if he didn't make the call, perhaps whatever waited on the end of the line would go away on its own, perhaps he was too inebriated and he was projecting his fear and his drunkenness onto her, and perhaps it wasn't fear in her voice, perhaps she missed him. How long had he gone without speaking to her? What month was it? He didn't realize it was two days until Christmas, although the snow on the ground outside and the hum of the furnace revealed it was the coldest part of the year.

I dialed six numbers / one more to go
Been a long time / since we've said hello

Jody opened his worried eyes and pressed the seventh number. Frost ravaged the landscape beyond the window. The dusty clock on the dusty dresser said it was a quarter till six, but he wasn't sure whether it was a.m. or p.m., not that it mattered. He waited, receiver in hand. A drunken Irene answered after the fourth ring and the world turned around them. Her answering machine picked up at the same time she did, and so she battled her own voice, not waiting for the recording to stop, struggling to talk over it, not realizing it was her own self she was competing with.

The recording eventually ended with a long monotone. *Leave a message after the beep.*

"Mom."

"Jody? I'm surry this friggin' machine iza nightmare. I dunno howda turnit off. I just haveda whey for the friggin' bleep

74

—the friggin' *beep*," Irene corrected herself as if it mattered, her words melding together.

"Mom—I got your message. What's going on?"

"Jody, I needa taltah yah. Honey kin you come home?"

"I am home—in Dayton. You want me to go to Midville?"

"Yes. Kin you come home so I—"

"Sure, what's going on?"

He heard her burst into tears on the other end. The crying gradually became hysterical as she spat panicked, high-pitched, incoherent syllables that didn't form words, let alone sentences. He let her rant continue for a few moments, attempting to discern some kind of meaning from the few words he could make out. As her hysteria ebbed and her volume softened a bit, he heard the words "so scared" and "don't know what to do."

"Mom. Listen. I'm going to drive down there. You stay put."

"… just so scared …"

"Mom, mom, I can't understand you. I'll be there in a few. Wait there. Don't try to go anywhere. We'll figure it out."

He made the familiar forty-five minute journey to Midville, although this time it felt like he was headed down a road he didn't know. Wide-eyed, he piloted the two-lane highway that connected the two cities. The luminous intensity of the sky weakened, proving it was in fact evening, giving way to a moonless night. He saw duplicates of the few cars on the roads in front of him, listening to the white hum of the night. The road ahead extended into the horizon and connected to the drained sky. He drove south, confined only by the empty cornfields shivering around him, a depleted landscape, naked and exposed. An unemployed scarecrow stood perched in one of the barren fields, waiting to do what he was meant to do with his life. Jody's car seemed self-propelled this evening, disassociated from his physical body. Muscle memory did much of the work required to maneuver the one-ton heap of machinery along the snowplowed Ohio roads. The vehicle moved slowly but with intent, remaining focused in its lane—and when he arrived in Midville, Jody regained control of the wheel, sliding back into his life, sobered by the weight in his chest.

Knowing that drinking had likely become more important than eating, Jody stopped at Burger King, purchased burgers and fries for the two of them. The brunette behind the restaurant's counter was sixteen, maybe seventeen, with freckles, a tiny body, and small tits that formed perfect little bumps under her tightly tucked shirt. Jody slid his sunglasses down the bridge of his nose, peered at her, holding her gaze. She looked nervous when he flirted with her, as though maybe she wanted to flirt back but wasn't entirely sure whether she was allowed, or maybe she was weirded out by this aging man. Contact with this girl sobered him, clearing his thoughts, removing his mind from the possibilities ahead. In the company of back and forth glances with this girl, he waited for his food until it arrived in a logoed white paper bag: two individually wrapped burgers and two cartons of french fries and two napkins and *fuck she forgot the goddamn ketchup packets*. And when he left the restaurant the second time, the white bag also contained a stack of napkins and several handfuls of ketchup packets and the teenage girl's phone number on the back of a napkin, which he quickly crumpled and tossed in the waste can near the exit.

Jody parallel-parked on the street and climbed the three steps to his mother's apartment, grease-stained bag in tow. He knocked on the door and waited, and when she didn't answer, he found a key waiting under an eighteen-inch statue of the Virgin Mary near the side door. He unlocked the lock, hid the key back under the Virgin, and cautiously opened the door to her apartment, exposing its contents to the brisk winter winds beyond the building's wood and brick walls. As he entered the apartment, its old floors creaked under the weight of shared discontent. The front door opened to the diningroom with capacious ceilings and damaged antique furniture from various eras, giving a line of sight through an archway to an open livingroom with its large windows framing a view of the nighttime street, walls adorned with framed photographs, an ivory sofa with fresh red-wine stains, and a coffeetable supporting an ashtray brimming with butts and several empty wine bottles. Irene was slouched on the sofa in a coma-like sleep, wearing a patterned bathrobe and mismatched socks and nothing else, her head tilted back, mouth wide open, robe slightly undone, exposing her left breast to current company, which besides Jody included only her small dog, Sera (shortened literally from *Serotonin*), who was sleeping beside Irene in an eerily similar position—head back, mouth open, furry belly exposed, catatonic. The other side of the diningroom contained two doors, one that led to Irene's bedroom and bathroom; the other, to the kitchen. Both doors were closed. The air inside the apartment was stale and dry and hazy with cigarette smoke.

Walked in the door / everything had changed
Sat there in front of me / a thousand miles away
A new look in your eyes / I knew it then
This moment / the beginning of the end

He set the fast-food bag on one of several doilies on the diningroom table next to three stacks of unopened mail and stepped slowly through the rooms. A single light shone in the livingroom—a bright lamp in the corner opposite Irene. It was not a room designed for an alcoholic—a failed room with unforgiving hard surfaces and rough edges and clumsy obstacles scattered throughout, waiting to be tripped over or fallen into. He sat in a wooden chair next to this white-haired woman, waking Serotonin slightly. The tiny dog rustled a bit, licking her lips and wagging her tail lazily, remembering Jody from infrequent visits over the years.

He petted the dog and noticed a difference in Irene. How long had she been drinking? Her body looked different, frailer, slightly foreign and unfamiliar. She was thinner than ever—thrust into metamorphosis, the accelerated change of uncontrollable events. He tried to wake her with some calming words, but she remained unconscious. After a few minutes sitting there, Jody repeating kind words to soothe his mother, waiting on her to respond, she began making barely audible sounds—those incoherent words people say when they talk in their sleep. She was having an animated conversation with someone in her dream—a man named Dan—in which nearly every word was inaudible, except Jody thought he heard her say the word "kegels" more than once, uncertain of its context or relevance. She looked like she hadn't been eating, like the weight of whatever was troubling her was what was important now, and all those other things—tasks, errands, chores, bills, meals—had lost their significance somewhere along the way. A cigarette was still burning in the overflowing ashtray on the coffeetable, an inch and a half of ash at its tip.

After waiting a moment for something to happen, though he didn't know exactly what he was hoping for, he carried the small, old woman to her bedroom and placed her on her bed and retreated to the sofa for the night. Before he closed his eyes he looked out the window and felt threatened by the darkness beyond its panes. He closed his eyes and waited for sleep, the world lost inside him.

Throughout the night he took the dreams as they came, sorting through them one by one, each one more real and more intense than the previous. Most vivid was a dream of his drive to Midville through the same snow-laden fields, down the same empty roads, with the same drained sky in its twilight, although the sky itself appeared nearer the earth now, sprawled in stardust and angst. He drove faster than his instruments should've allowed. The arc lamps on the road were all switched off, forcing him to rely on his natural instincts and the vehicle's high beams to illuminate his journey. And when the headlights began to flicker, and the sky blackened as the night won its battle against the day, he couldn't see where to turn or what to do. His instincts failed him. The needle on the dash read empty but the journey into the darkness didn't stop, and then the car seemed to buckle beneath him and the driving surface changed as if he had veered off the road, making it impossible to know which way was the right way and which way was not. He couldn't've planned for this. He clutched the steering wheel with both hands and jammed the footbrake as hard as he could, waiting for God's wrath and hoping to make it to the other side with the least amount of damage possible. The sound of the cataclysm didn't possess any of the shrieks or metal-on-metal tearing he had expected, just the symphonic sounds of broken glass, windows shattering around him in beautiful dissonance, disobeying the physical laws of the car crash, shattering before impact, breaking in preparation for the collision, not waiting for the accident but bracing for it. There was a cross of flowers on the roadside. And then everything was still, and in the darkness someone was opening the door for him. It was the out-of-work scarecrow he'd seen in the vacant fields during the twilight. As he got out of the car there was a sternness of judgment in the barrens, shades of flamed earth under dimmed skies. One of the road's arc lamps flickered on, casting shadows on the bleached fields around them. Somehow the front of the car had wrapped itself around a telephone pole, the hood was mangled, the rise of smoke and the steam of half-a-dozen fluids plumed from the engine, reaching for the arc lamp and beyond, to the sky and the stars and whatever else was out there in the heavens spectating this event. His hands were bleeding and he couldn't form a clear picture of what had happened. It was cold. He wondered whether it was supposed to be this cold. The scarecrow stood next to him, next to the wreckage, and said, "You were going in the wrong direction." It was impossible for Jody to disagree.

When he awoke, he woke to sunlight and cigarette smoke and Serotonin. Besides the vivid car crash, he didn't recall any of the other digressions that had occurred while his body was sprawled out on the sofa. This moment felt like the moment after the accident, staring back at the wreckage.

The first day brought with it a plan. The plan was to wait, to have no plan at all, to take in the events as they occurred, to react accordingly. This plan emptied his mind and made him feel the solitude of this place. The apartment pulsed with daylight and time. Irene was awake, making soft clanging noises somewhere out of sight, rustling items in a kitchen drawer. The two clocks in the livingroom contradicted each other and Jody didn't bother to check to see which was correct, or whether either was correct, because that wasn't part of the plan. The plan didn't account for time, at least not in the sense brought forth by clocks on apartment walls. If the plan *did* allow for time, it did so in a different way—the way of the moment, *this* moment, for this moment *was* time, wasn't it? The plan accounted for the time it took to wait for the next moment—waiting required this kind of time, not clock time, but real time, real-life time, a lifetime of real time. The happenings of the world around the apartment, this was the kind of time the plan accounted for.

What is time? How much time is a long time? Jody rubbed his eyes and ran his fingers through his hair, looking around the room for anything that resembled a reality less bleak, feeling time go by, viscerally, even painfully. When time stops, so do we. It's something that no one understands, but it unfolds into the seams of being, passing through us, making and shaping us, defining our existence. We are made of time; it is the force that tells us who we are. Jody closed his eyes and he could feel it.

Irene came into view as she entered the diningroom, wearing a different stained bathrobe, holding a large plastic cup. A cigarette dangled from her lip, lit haphazardly, the ash uneven at the tip. She was either still buzzed from the night before or was on her way to the day's oblivion. Or both.

"Honey, I made you some coffee. It's in the pot. I'd make you some breakfast, but I'm afraid I'm out of everything," she said in a tone that welcomed him home. *Welcome back to the chaos, it's been waiting for you.*

Jody nodded a *thank you* and sat up.

"You don't look anything like yourself," Irene said, staring at him with glazed eyes.

"How so?" Jody sat up straight, stiffly congruent with the cramped sofa.

"You look older."

"I am older. Every year Time betrays me."

"Not just older. You look wiser. You were always wise as a

child, you know." Her words were slurred, which made them sound slightly condescending.

He didn't feel any older at the time, but events during the coming months would change that. The uncertainty of the night before lingered. Serotonin entered the room briefly and vied for Jody's attention. He put his hand on Serotonin to pacify her and keep her at bay. This moment was something he needed to feel without her. He went to the bathroom and then to the kitchen, and when he returned Irene was on the sofa next to her dog. The air reeked of bad tidings. Jody set his coffee on the table and sat in the chair nearest his mother. They talked. She told him about the cancer.

People don't know how to love the ones they love until they disappear from their lives. The next eight months birthed a new Jody Grafton, from a man who was lost without knowing he was lost—wandering perpetually through time, waiting for something to happen—to a man who was looking for a new self. Not a better man, but a different man was birthed, developing through trial and error, embracing the darkness to find the light. These dark months were filled with vast indiscretions and myriad emotions he'd never experienced on the surface, emotions he'd locked inside himself until now: fear, depression, loneliness. The truth, when brought to the surface, was hard to handle.

Later that year, in the final days of summer, the leaves resisted the change of color, and Irene resisted the division of cells as they metastasized beyond her lungs to other vital organs and, eventually, to her brain. And on September 13th, 2009, in a hospice room in Dayton, Ohio, Jody Grafton cried for the first time in his adult life.

Only tears can describe / the words I can't explain
For the first time / they're streaming down my face
Even though you're gone / I'll never forget you
I wish you were here / I'm sorry, I miss you

Jody finished writing the words and signed his name at the bottom of the page, and then he fished himself out of the song and looked ahead and saw an entirely new world in the foreground now. The past was the past. The rain stopped and a small, clear puddle had accumulated nearby. A bird landed on the Brooklyn rooftop, warbling a melody, hinting at a new song.

THE LONELIEST MAN

The Troubled Man stood naked in the cold room, a bedroom he'd never occupied before, feeling what it meant to be alive, looking out a window as last light drained from the lavender sky onto the suburban sprawl; onto dense, tidy flowerbeds; onto tool sheds and undone yard work; onto rows of indistinguishable houses with dull, tan siding, houses separated at precise intervals by well-kept side yards and three-year-old birch trees held stable by ropes and wood planks too young and too fragile to withstand the elements on their own; onto neighboring houses in which sad families fought over TV remote controls and didn't talk to each other at the dinner table; onto this window and this room and past the Troubled Man; onto the frame on the dresser on the other side of the room containing a picture of an average-looking young man with his left arm around the young woman who was now lying in the bed behind the Troubled Man, both people in the picture wearing gold rings on the fourth finger of their left hands and smiling the magazine smiles people install on their faces for such photographs; onto the space behind the

Troubled Man—this room, the room over his shoulder—and onto the brown-eyed young woman halfway under a crinkled sheet in her bed, lying there beneath the shape of her body. She slept or rested or pretended to do both through closed eyes. This was his work now, in this dim room. He was here, and only here, disappeared from all prior venues, a blankness, a body erased of every past indiscretion. This was who he was. He became himself when he wasn't the other man, the man outside the walls of these bedrooms.

Blankets and pillows occupied the floor nearest the bed. The Troubled Man wanted a cigarette, but she had asked him not to smoke in here. He watched her breathe, wondering what she was thinking, whether she was asleep, what she was dreaming. She breathed deeply, slowly, but she wasn't at ease. Her breaths expanded and contracted her diaphragm underneath the sheets, a silent song. He felt a cruel satisfaction in the lull of her overwrought breaths. The sunlight began to give way to nightfall on the other side of the windowpanes. All at once a thousand blackbirds of spring erupted from their trees, forming distinct patterns in a thousand shades of black, flying into their secret night.

The world happens; it has to, so we can feel it.

The Troubled Man looked at himself in the mirror above the vanity. Strange that it's called a vanity, that such an object can predict its honest use. He stared at himself with a kind of solemn self-absorption, a harmony within discord, a satisfaction within discontent.

The Troubled Man returned to the bed, nudging the young woman's shoulders with the stubble of his chin, waking her from a false sleep, wedging them back into ecstasy, the language of thirst, their mouths ajar for tongues and nipples and fingers and flesh, a displacement of self, a false communion, a giving-in to their sins, two bodies in a room, separated by deep dimensions. How strange the discontinuity.

There's a code in even the simplest acts of physical intimacy, a code that tells the minds and flesh and nerve-endings involved what's happening between the two bodies, an unspoken, undefinable connection. This was missing from the Troubled Man's interactions with these women—with *this* woman. He lost touch with them—with *her*. Even his gestures seemed marked by struggle. He lost interest sometimes, couldn't locate the precise rhythm or time cues or even the mutters and hums that pace the act of intercourse. Just two bodies in a room, in a state of perpetual collapse, doing what bodies do, fucking, not making love, everything raw in the moment, open-wounded.

After she came, he came, lying there in anxious afterglow. The Troubled Man's thoughts drifted toward his ex-wife, as they often did, toward the mess he'd made.

Perhaps she didn't mind the mess. This couldn't be true. Or could it? After all, his wife had been a forgiving woman, an understanding woman who didn't want her husband to feel the pain he felt. She had wanted only the best for him—wanted to *be* the best for him—and had been willing to go to great lengths to help him be the good man that she knew he was. But after a year of excessive drinking and unnecessary arguments and unwinnable fights, her patience dwindled, and she told him she was leaving if he didn't stop drinking. And when he did stop drinking, she even forgave his first indiscretion, chalking it up to his mother's death, his unhappy career, his tormented childhood, his misguided life.

So it was the Troubled Man who left instead. It was he who walked away self-deprecatingly—knowing she was too good for him, knowing he didn't deserve her, knowing she deserved someone better. He thought maybe she knew about him all along, that he was going to do this. It was a thing he carried with him, not a question of chemicals in his brain, it was *him* who he was. They had been two people with one life and it had been *his* life. But she was content with that life—all she wanted was him. And all he wanted was to find what he was looking for; he wasn't sure what that was, but he thought he'd recognize it when he found it.

During the months immediately following his marriage, the Troubled Man had created his own totalitarian regime, one in which he was the dictator and also the oppressed people, a perfectly solipsistic tyranny. And within the confines of his self-inflicted pain, he found the women to bandage his wounds. He found them wherever he could: at bars, at restaurants, at coffeeshops, at friends' houses, wherever. If a woman was near, it was his obligation to invite her into his world, if just for an evening. And so there was A—— and N—— and A—— and T —— and M—— and S—— and C—— and N—— and L—— and a handful of nameless others. One at a time, two bodies in a room.

The Troubled Man moved through these bedrooms uneasily. He hated who he was outside these rooms, but inside this was him at his fundament—cold, mammalian, hard-hearted. But he was pleased inside these rooms, pleased only in the moment though—*at least I won't be alone tonight*. He never felt fulfilled, never felt satisfied with this life, a life of acting on impulse, a life without love, whatever that word meant. He spent time looking into their eyes during the act itself, searching for something, a connection, a feeling of something more than what it was. Lying next to them afterward, he breathed the heat of their merciful dreams, wondering who they were, callously pondering the truth he'd never know, because this is the secret that sleep protects in its natural layers and folds. Above all, he wanted them to love him, to need him in ways he didn't need them. And if he was able to love, then he loved all these women. But he didn't know this feeling, this sentiment, this experience outside these rooms with two bodies doing what two bodies do, making everything foggy. He knew it was foolish to examine everything so closely. It was easier to live in the fog. But he was a fool a thousand times, a fool every day of his existence.

Sometimes the Troubled Man got them to talk a little, to converse with him. But these women were not eager to talk beyond the words necessary to initiate the act—this was, after all, a reciprocal deed, pleasure for pleasure, pain for pain, pleasure to escape a particular kind of pain, the pain of feeling alone, and yet these transgressions did just that: they made him feel alone.

And now he lay here, in this room, in this bed, with this young woman, basking in the aftermath. And he was himself. Pleasure for pleasure, offering touches and calming sounds, two bodies in a room.

Outside, a car door shut, and the woman jumped out of bed with a startled face. She shuffled hurriedly toward the window, still tangled in orgasm and in the fabric of the sheets. Her buttocks jiggled. The Troubled Man liked how she looked when she panicked—vulnerable, overwhelmed by her poor decisions. Misery encourages others to pull up a chair and stay a while. She looked out the window and said it was her husband and that he wasn't supposed to be home until Tuesday night, and the Troubled Man calmly reminded her that it *was* in fact Tuesday night now and this alarmed her even more for some reason. She vomited some words, incoherent gibberish indicating he should be dressed, while she tossed blankets and pillows unsystematically onto the bed, cursing the ceiling and the walls and the air around her tremulous self.

The Troubled Man laughed to himself and pulled on his pants while the woman was pulling on all her clothes at once, searching her cortex for a story. *The mind tells us whatever story we want to believe.* The Troubled Man nearly had his shirt over his head, covering most of his colorful tattoos, when the man from the framed photo walked into the room, his puzzled expression mirroring his words: *What are you doing in my fucking room?*

BLACK & WHITE & SHADES OF GRAY

After high school, Jody Grafton moved from Midville to Dayton with his two best friends, Gray and Eric. At that point, all of Jody's closest friends were young black kids from his old neighborhood, even his adopted brother Gray, which instated Jody as a sort of honorary member of their community, accepted when others weren't, accepted as one of their own, a pale version of them.

Although they didn't have plans to attend college, the trio spent a generous chunk of their time near the University of Dayton, a few miles from their apartment on the other side of the river. Lazy afternoons were spent stalking the near-campus streets, flirting with college freshwomen who wore laughably short shorts whenever the temperature exceeded sixty degrees, sneaking into dorm rooms and having unprotected sex with faux-Catholic girls who were themselves having unprotected sex with other guys. Eric was worst of all: he had a habit of telling every attractive girl he slept with that she was *the one* and then not calling her after the first night.

There appeared to be two seasons in Ohio: winter and construction. Thanks to what must have been a No Road Left Unpaved stimulus package, there was construction everywhere in 1999, mostly east of the river. Half the roads in the city were in various stages of deconstruction or reconstruction, from pothole-filling mini-projects to orange-cone-lined multi-month lane-widening undertakings. The roads in Jody's neighborhood could've used some love from one or two of those ventures. Every time the three of them piled into Jody's ramshackle Buick Regal, its shocks ached and clanged as they drove over massive potholes west of the river. Some of those potholes had potholes within the pothole, kind of resembling one of those strange M.C. Escher sketches that awed Jody as a child. Every day they hopped into that rust-white Regal and trekked across those poorly maintained streets, headed east across the saprogenic Great Miami River, swerving and missing each gaping hole in the road, including one massive pothole in front of a grim, fenced building with *Dayton Division of Street Maintenance* printed on its facade.

When they returned home each night—or early in the morning before the sun rose behind them—the person who was closest to sober would assume the driver's seat and motor across the stale river. A sign on the darker side of the bridge displayed their neighborhood's name, *Dayton View*, the city skyline in the rearview for only a few seconds, and then as the cityscape dematerialized, empty storefronts appeared along West Third Street, followed by several barred liquor stores, a beauty supply shop, and a Dollar General with a large "going out of business" banner draped below the building's exterior signage even though it had been closed for months.

Jody, Gray, and Eric's tumbledown three-bedroom

apartment was on this side of the river, and although it was less than two miles from the university, the two neighborhoods were worlds apart. It's stunning the difference a mile and a river can make. Unlike the near-campus housing, their neighborhood was relatively cheap and was conveniently located close to rundown bars and liquor stores and greasy soul-food restaurants and open-air drug trafficking.

The Great Miami River, which runs roughly parallel to I-75, the city's main interstate, served as a modern Mason-Dixon Line, separating the vastly black westside from the mostly white eastside. Their neighborhood was called Dayton View, although save for one small sliver on the edge of the neighborhood, there was no view of Dayton here, at least not the tall-building-strewn downtown skyline one might expect to see in a place with such a moniker, and yet the view was an inverted one, a view of a different side of the city, the limbic portion of the other side of Dayton, the edge of west Dayton, a darker place, a sore on the heart of Ohio.

To make money that spring, Jody and Eric played guitar at local bars and pizza parlors, singing vapid renditions of mid- and late-nineties rock cover songs, scraping up enough tip money to pay past-due utility bills before their final suspension-of-service notices. Meanwhile, Gray reconnected with an old friend from their old Midville neighborhood, a young man named Rob Jackson, who was two years older than the trio and was affectionately known in their old neighborhood as "Nigga Rob," which everyone pronounced as one word: "Niccarob."

Niccarob had dropped out of high school at fifteen after being arrested for driving without a license, possession of an unregistered firearm, possession of half a pound of marijuana with the intent to distribute, possession of eighteen grams of crack cocaine with the intent to distribute, possession of alcohol by a minor, open container, and changing lanes without signaling, all of which occurred in the same traffic stop by an officer of the Midville Police Department. Because of his age, he spent only six months in Juvenile Detention, where he learned to be more careful with future felonies. After being released on probation at sixteen, he had discovered the errors of his ways. He personally embraced the drug dealer's apothegm *don't get high off your own supply*. No more drugs, no more alcohol—just a clean system, a clear mind, and increased revenues. Within a week of his release, he was back on the block selling marijuana and crack cocaine and powder cocaine and prescription pills to willing buyers. He netted more than a thousand dollars a week in cash, but this time he took precautions. He intentionally avoided growing his business too fast; he refused to take on new customers unless another customer vouched for them; he avoided run-ins with the law by avoiding neighborhood do-gooders who would call the police at the sight of any suspicious activity; he stopped hanging out in all the local hot spots in which he used to linger—the park benches, the popular corners, the neighborhood party houses, and the parking lot of the local Section 8 housing units were all off limits. In many ways, he became a ghost. For a year, Niccarob kept to himself and steadily grew his business. By seventeen he had a storage locker on the edge of town containing nearly a hundred thousand dollars in cash. He continued to stay out of the limelight, living in a small two-bedroom house he rented in the same Midville neighborhood in which he was raised.

Midville was a blue-collar city. Its primary industries were steel manufacturing and soda bottling, which locals referred to as "hard steelin' and pop bottlin'." Most of its citizenry were white lower-middle-class folks who had little more ambition than to earn a paycheck every other Friday and spend it on ephemeral comforts that took the edge off an already dull life.

The poorest neighborhood in Midville was a small twenty-block neighborhood north of Warren Street called Pleasant Park, a primarily black neighborhood on the northside of the city's dilapidated downtown. Pleasant Park was named after the largest street that ran through the neighborhood, not the demeanor of its residents. The neighborhood encircled a large park that held the same name as the neighborhood. Much of the neighborhood's youth occupied their days in Pleasant Park's Pleasant Park, playing basketball and drinking from rusty water fountains during the hot and hazy summers, bundling up in oversized goose-down coats and sitting on park benches during the cold and snowy winters. Pleasant Park the neighborhood was easy to get into but hard to leave. There were five streets providing five points of entry into the neighborhood, three of which were one-way streets, which meant there were only two ways to get out of the neighborhood.

By eighteen, Niccarob was determined to avoid run-ins with the law. He traded his Lexus SUV for a clean-but-far-less-flashy Toyota Avalon. He earned his G.E.D. and enrolled in community college, learning business finance and macro- and microeconomics, appreciating the principles of the inelasticity of demand that inherently characterized his products. Over time, he distanced himself from his customers by establishing a small network of trusted employees, a handful of younger guys from the neighborhood, drug dealers with names like Patch, Big Will, Mook, Lil' B, J-9, and C-Pain, who sold Niccarob's products while he slipped quietly into the background. He purchased two local businesses—a coin-operated laundromat and a dry cleaners, both of which were lucky to break even, even on a good month —into which he funneled his illegitimate cash, showing a large but not unreasonable profit from both businesses, paying taxes on the income, walking away with clean money. He moved any extra cash out of the storage lockers and divided it amongst multiple storage facilities in nearby towns. He paid the remaining debt on his grandmother's house and bought her a new car. She was, after all, the woman who'd raised him, and he wanted her taken care of.

In every way he could, Niccarob stayed off the radar. But certain situations were unavoidable. He had no real competition in Midville; sure, there were petty hustlers who sold weed or pills to their friends, but no one moved any weight into the city. Everyone was happy with the setup: the corner dealers made enough money, the crime stayed low, and the locals appreciated the quality of their purchases. He had inadvertently established what one of his textbooks called a "local monopoly." His business was a utility of sorts—gas, electric, cable TV, beer, and narcotics; these were the things on which Midvillians depended to get through the drudgery of their day-to-day lives, and he was happy to provide at least one good or service they demanded. His economics 301 class taught him about the fundamental problems of a monopoly with respect to new competition in the marketplace. A flood of competition would necessarily result in lower product prices, reductions in force, and would obviously bring unwanted attention to his business. This was unacceptable. So when a couple dope dealers from Cincinnati tried to move their product into Midville, he had to react quickly and firmly.

The Cincinnatians first approached a few of the guys on Niccarob's crew, offering them a larger cut of sales if they took on their product instead of his. None of his crew took the bait and the out-of-towners left empty-handed. When they returned to Pleasant Park a week later, there were four of them this time, and they set up shop on their own at the edge of the park. From their point of view, selling in this neighborhood was easy.

Within an hour, Niccarob caught wind of their presence and made a rare personal appearance that night as the four new faces sold their product to *his* customers in *his* park in *his* neighborhood in *his* city. Under a half-torn moon, in the swell of the midnight summer heat, he walked by himself to the park, which was empty other than two of his dealers sitting on benches as well as two teenage civilians—two youngsters named Jody and Gray, both sixteen at the time—who occupied another bench on the other side of the park, loitering underneath the streetlights illuminating the impending encounter.

Carrying the weight of his reputation on his back, Niccarob strolled through the park's damp grass, over an empty basketball court, and between sets of uninhabited swings. A dark silence engulfed the park. The crickets became more articulate amongst the hush. He continued his stroll toward the four unfamiliar faces until he stood a few feet from the group's largest man, a tall dark-skinned man wearing a tight white tank-top that exposed his large biceps. The man was nearly a foot taller than Niccarob, who stood directly in front of the man, looking up at him in a brief moment of wordlessness while the other three men inched closer to see what was going on.

"Do you know who I am?" Niccarob asked calmly, looking up at the man into his dark eyes.

"What?" The big man laughed off this question, but shifted his eyes toward his comrades and looked a little uneasy at this ballsy approach.

"Do you know who I am?" He repeated in the same unruffled tone.

"Nigga, I don't give a fuck who—"

The echo of a single gunshot overtook the silence before the man could finish his sentence. The other three men scattered, one yelled "Oh shit!" in a panicked tone. Niccarob's two dealers leapt off their benches and disappeared into the night. Jody and Gray followed suit, vanishing into an alley, running through two blocks of fenced backyards until they reached their house, their mother passed out on the couch, a cigarette still burning in her ashtray.

Minutes later, sirens played in the distance, but by then the park was empty, except for the body lying on the sidewalk at the park's edge.

A tasteless picture of coagulated bloodstains and pink brain matter and a chalk outline on the sidewalk made the front page of the *Midville Star*, which noted that the MPD was "investigating the homicide," but there were currently "no suspects and no eye-witnesses to the brutal slaying." That had been the only murder Jody and Gray had ever witnessed. No one from the neighborhood talked about it publicly, but almost everyone knew who was responsible.

Three years later it was Gray who approached Niccarob about selling some product, mostly marijuana, on consignment, to local college kids in Dayton. A harmless crime, simply supplying a pent-up demand, providing a convenient service to the local college community. After all, they were going to get it somewhere, weren't they? Besides, he was broke, and they needed rent money. Jody was indifferent to this new business venture, but he told his brother he'd help if he needed it. Eric, on the other hand, vehemently opposed any such dealings and refused to play a role in it. Niccarob agreed to front Gray a pound of weed but also asked him to take two ounces of cocaine, noting that, "Coke is what a lot of those Catholic kids are into."

Boy was he right.

Within three months, Gray and Jody set the campus afire. They established an efficient process that included pagers, pay phones, and a system of codes for the college kids to use when "ordering" their drugs. They handed out free samples in bar bathrooms and at frat parties and any other social event at which college kids congregated. The quality of their drugs was better than most. The locals started referring to their coke as Red Sky (because of the miniature red ziplock bags they used to package the stuff) and to their weed as Green Sky (mainly because you could buy it off the same guys who sold the Red Sky coke).

Summer break rolled around. All the college kids were packing up their dorms. Gray and Jody had saved over ten thousand dollars after paying their regular bills and blowing a few grand on stuff they didn't remember spending money on. It was the summer of a new millennium, only a year after they graduated high school, and they were making more money than any of their parents had ever made. With their newfound success, they allowed their friend Eric to continue to freeload, living essentially rent-free at their apartment. Eric continued to play music at local gigs and flirt with the girls Jody and Gray brought home (Gray even suspected that Eric was sleeping with his main girl, though he couldn't prove it), but Jody stopped paying him much attention; he was too busy to play music with Eric, too busy being a new kind of local celebrity: the beloved neighborhood drug dealer, the man who, for a small fee, had all the answers.

Surprisingly, the summer didn't bring the slowdown in

business that Gray and Jody had anticipated. Many of the UD kids stuck around, working tedious summer jobs and taking extra classes, and even the kids who left town started phoning in their orders, having product delivered directly to their doorstep via the United States Postal Service. The quality of Niccarob's product was so good—and Gray and Jody were shockingly reliable entrepreneurs—that the college kids preferred to pay the fifty-dollar "handling fee" to have Red Sky and/or Green Sky mailed to them. And it turned out that Uncle Sam was an incredibly competent drug trafficker, guaranteeing overnight delivery for less than fifteen dollars.

Within four short months, Gray and Jody quickly became a very profitable extension of Niccarob's Midville crew. A sort of satellite office. This radical change was strange for the duo, a weird kind of success that they knew they should be ashamed of, and perhaps were ashamed of deep down, but the facade of money and success and ostensible power masked the shame whenever it tried to peek its ugly head through to the surface. They found temporary solace in their new status. They were suddenly important to a large group of people who couldn't've cared less about them just four months earlier, and in all honesty still wouldn't've cared much about them had they not been the suppliers of certain short-term remedies in little red plastic baggies, and so they felt wanted, an exciting, gratifying feeling, which only increased their need to continue the charade. They were trapped by the tyranny of being cool.

Niccarob's rapaciousness shined that summer. He encouraged the duo to sell even more product, asking them to "ramp up their distribution" for the back-to-school madness that was around the corner. So *ramp up* they did. He gave Gray three pounds of marijuana and half a kilogram of cocaine on consignment, worth roughly thirty thousand dollars on the streets. Jody turned nineteen, catching up to his brother in age, and they sold the remainder of their existing product. The increased pressure to sell more felt like a fun challenge at the time, a corporate goal of sorts, so the duo started to branch out to nightclubs and bars, finding new customers within various new demographic segments. They started this expansion with a few biker bars and soon determined that Jody should handle those establishments on his own, given certain obvious marked incongruities in pigmentation between Gray and the bars' patrons. The strip of gay nightclubs downtown bore much more fruit than the biker bars, so their efforts shifted to those establishments. Jody didn't mind gay men, but Gray didn't take too kindly to being hit on by other guys. At first he didn't mind the overt acts of kindness—*Let me buy you a drink?* or *Who are you here with?*—but then when some thirty-something placed his hand on the back of Gray's hand at the restroom sink, Gray lunged at him with a roundhouse swing that broke the man's jaw and left him unconscious on the bathroom floor. They didn't return to that particular club after that night. But the other gay clubs were a goldmine, carrying in them a relatively affluent crowd, mostly males of varying ethnicities between ages twenty-one and fifty who loved to party, the perfect demographic, making things almost too easy, transactional even. The only way it could have been easier would've been if they were allowed to set up a checkout terminal and place tiny barcodes on their red packages for more expedient purchases and back-end inventory tracking and reconciliation. For a month, the pair of rugged nineteen-year-olds spent a lot of time in the gay clubs—three or four nights a week—making their rounds, giving samples to the doormen who ignored their age, introducing themselves to new clients, and establishing an ordering process that made everything easier on all parties.

If they were to plot their revenue stream over those five months on a PowerPoint chart, the arrow would have pointed up and to the right—the corporate executive's ultimate desire—and the promise of continued upward movement was remarkably positive. At that point it was nearly impossible for them not to increase profits. With more and more cash coming in, Gray decided to purchase a new car; partially because he was tired of his current car overheating and breaking down and making him look like he didn't have any money, and partially because he wanted to ostentatiously display his newfound success to the world, to show them that things were different now, that he was no longer the Gray of yesteryear. His new car was a large, gently used 1984 Chevrolet Caprice Classic that he purchased in impeccable condition for four thousand dollars cash from a blue-haired lady whose husband had recently kicked the bucket. With less than sixty thousand miles, it appeared that the husband had rarely driven the car and that it spent the vast majority of its time resting in their garage, waiting to be taken on short trips to the grocery store or the doctor's office or Sunday church service. With the car still sporting temporary tags, Gray had the windows tinted with limousine tint so dark that people on the outside couldn't see in the windows even with their faces against the glass and their hands cupped around their ears. He dropped two grand on a deep-purple paint job with gold flakes that shimmered in the summer sun. He installed an unnecessarily loud stereo system, complete with a hundred-disc CD changer, an in-dash TV monitor, and ten speakers, two of which were large fifteen-inch subwoofers that made the trunk rattle uncontrollably when the music was going. And to top it all off, he purchased hundred-spoke gold Dayton rims with whitewall Vogue tires.

"Now all you need is a bumpersticker that says 'I'm a drug dealer,'" Jody said when he first saw the vehicle.

"Ain't nobody gonna think I'm a drug dealer because of my car," was the only thing Gray could think to reply.

"But you *are* a drug dealer."

"So what, it's just a car."

"Look, all I'm saying is that we have a good thing going, and your Barneymobile might bring some attention we don't need."

"It's not a big deal, Jody. Besides, didn't you go out and spend a bunch of money on stuff you wanted?"

"Yeah, I bought two vintage guitars."

"For how much?

"Like five or six grand."

"For a couple *guitars*? See, and aren't people going to ask you how you afforded those. What are you going to say when they do?"

"It's a bit different and you know it."

"Whatever. Seems the same to me."

"And what's with the bling, man?" Jody said, pointing at Gray's new gold chain overtop his crisp new clothes. "A gold chain and a bunch of new Polo and Tommy Hilfiger gear?" It was a new kind of luxury that he wasn't used to, a pan-seared opulence, blackened by the never-ending desire to consume more and more stuff outside of one's self, a desire that was, by definition, impossible to make someone fulfilled, to make someone happy on the inside.

"What's the big deal with buying some new clothes?" Gray asked.

"I'm just saying. We have a good thing going. No need to rock the boat."

"We don't need to pretend like we're broke and living back in Midville either."

"I agree. We just need to be careful is all I'm saying."

"I am being careful. It's me that got us this whole set up with Niccarob in the first place, isn't it?"

"I never said you didn't. I'm just trying to look out for—"

"You're not looking out for me if you're worried about me buying a few new shirts. Didn't you buy some new clothes too?"

"I bought some white teeshirts from Walmart if that's what you're talking about," Jody replied.

"What about those sunglasses you're wearing? They look expensive. How much they set you back?"

"Look, I'm not trying to stand here and argue with you. I'm just making a few observations. We might want to slow down is all I'm saying."

"Alright, whatever man."

And with this argument, Jody knew that Gray didn't know how to handle the responsibilities of their new income. He knew their paths were diverging right before their eyes, even if Gray didn't yet acknowledge it, and for the first time since their childhood, Jody felt like they were growing apart, like the money and the possessions could change a man in ways that nothing else could (except maybe addictions like alcohol or drugs or sex). But before their paths could bifurcate too drastically, everything was about to change.

On the night of July 10th, Gray drove them from their apartment to the downtown district in which the gay nightclubs were situated, Jody sat in the passenger seat, listening to the bass from Gray's music as it rattled the car's trunk and shook its dark windows. Jody was the first to notice the red and blue lights flashing hysterically in the passenger-side rearview mirror. *Objects in the mirror are closer than they appear.* He quickly turned down the music using one of the knobs on the stereo's complex control panel.

"What is you doing? That's my shit right there," Gray said, still moving his head rhythmically to the now nonexistent beat.

"PO-leece."

"What? Shit!"

"It's cool, you probably just forgot to use your turn signal or something."

"No, no, no. No!" Gray's normally steadfast voice possessed an unfamiliar panic. "This isn't happening."

"What? What's the big deal? Just play it cool."

"The shit's still in the trunk."

"What shit?" Jody asked, hoping it wasn't the *shit* he thought it was.

"Niccarob's shit. The shit I picked up last week."

"Last week? The half a key of blow?"

"Yeah. I didn't have a chance to take it to the spot yet."

Up until then, they had played it safe. They kept all their product stashed in a storage locker near campus so that, other than in transport, they never had drugs in their apartment or car. But with Gray's busy, consumerism-fueled week, he forgot to bring the latest round of drugs—by far their largest consignment to date—to the storage locker. Amid the hoarding of new treasures, Gray was unaware that he was heaping those items onto his own tomb.

"OK. We'll lock our free samples for the club in the glove box. They can't check it without a warrant," Jody said as he opened the glove compartment. Among a few stray papers and receipts, was a large black handgun. "What the hell is this?" he asked, not knowing that Gray owned a gun.

"What's it look like? It's a pistol."

"What? Why?" Jody slid off his sunglasses and stared at Gray.

"Gotta protect ourselves."

"You didn't tell me you got a gun."

"I just got it."

"But we don't need guns."

The lights were right behind them. Gray slowed the car and veered to the right side of the road. The Chevy rolled to a stop. The cop's spotlight and flashing red-and-blue strobes flooded the vehicle with light so bright that Jody could have read a book in the passenger seat. They both tossed their tiny baggies of Red Sky and Green Sky into the glove box and locked it.

"OK. That's locked. The trunk is locked. Just play it cool," Jody said these words to try to calm himself as much as to try to calm his brother. But the look that broke across Gray's features told another story.

"Look. We'll stick to your plan," Gray said. "Keep everything locked. But if that doesn't work and if we go down for this, it's all on me man. You didn't know nothin' about nothin'. I was just giving you a ride." This was the Gray that Jody knew, the man who broke away from his newfound lust for material items and protected his little brother. Growing up, Gray had always been the toughest kid Jody knew, and he had always gone to great lengths to protect his little brother. That reality returned now and Gray looked calm, at ease, at peace with the world around him. He seemed suddenly aware of the consequences of his actions, the result of lusting after everything he had lusted after. The money. The power. The neighborhood fame. The desire to be loved without contributing to others. These were the sins he would pay for. He knew this now, even before the police officer walked to his tinted window with his service revolver drawn, pointed at Gray's head an inch from the glass.

People don't know how to love the ones they love until they disappear from their lives. And a decade after his brother was swept away, Jody Grafton looked out at the world from this Brooklyn rooftop and penciled the lyrics to express his feelings:

I've carried this load / nearly broke my back
Ran with the Devil / I'm never going back
Now you're gone / I'll never forget the day
Amidst darkness / slipping through the Gray

A THOUSAND MILES AWAY

The Troubled Man was disgusted by the look on her face. She wore an expression that said *it's so wonderful to see you*. He wasn't disgusted by the actual look so much as he was by his reaction to the look: apathetic, disinterested, careless.

How could I love someone and treat her like this?

But no matter how hard he tried, he didn't want her anymore. He desperately *wanted* to want her, but he couldn't force himself any longer.

These days lacked a particular flavor. The Troubled Man arrived home late that afternoon with beer on his breath. His wife had spent the day cleaning their home, removing every hidden flecklet of dust from every dark corner in their oversized house, a chore she did for him, not herself. The kitchen was immaculate. They could've eaten dinner off the floor that evening.

They sat at the same diningroom table they'd sat at a thousand times before, alone together. A radio played softly in the next room, circulating with unspoken tension, adding ambience to the air. A singer's voice sang about the Troubled Man's sorrows.

The Troubled Man didn't know how else to say it. He told her he was leaving. He told her everything. An 8" x 10" bride-and-groom photo sat in a shiny metallic picture frame on the dust-free shelf behind her. They'd received the frame as a wedding gift nearly eight years earlier.

"You couldn't have waited until after our anniversary to tell me this?" she said with tears falling at an increasing rate.

The Troubled Man clutched the edges of the table, bracing himself for whatever emotions would work themselves into the room. He wasn't a crier but he felt it coming, he couldn't control it.

"I'm sorry," the Troubled Man said.

"You're sorry?"

"Yes. I'm sorry. I don't know what else to say at this point." He had said it so many times in the past—apologizing for being himself, apologizing for his actions, apologizing for apologizing —that the words meant nothing by now, empty, weightless words, like saying your own name over and over until it became a meaningless sound. He knew his *sorry* couldn't fix her broken heart. If you're careless with something for long enough, it breaks.

The curtains were drawn and it was dark outside and the light above the kitchen table was dimmed, providing the room with as much light as a large candle. The Troubled Man spent another fifteen minutes telling her that he loved her and that he still loves her but he doesn't want to be with her anymore, that he *can't* be with her anymore. His throat burned and he felt physically ill. He smelled a candle burning in the next room. Midnight Jasmine.

She said something—tried to say something—but her words were not leaving her mouth, they couldn't escape past her tears and heavy sobs. She sat there, openmouthed with incomprehension; thin strings of phlegm lined her lips as she weeped her gibberish. Eventually she stopped trying to speak and simply sobbed harder, louder. She was on the verge of hysteria and the Troubled Man wished there was something he could do, anything, but as usual he didn't know what to do; he didn't know how he should comfort her, how he could help. He was a problem solver, and this was a problem without clear resolution. He was reduced to the status of an infant, sitting there next to her, silent, feeling the tears in his own eyes now, reaching for her hand without a word, but she pulled back, jerked her hand away from his. People don't know how to love the ones they love until they disappear from their lives.

"I can't believe this is happening." She was finally able to push out these few words when the sobs subsided to a less-frantic level. She fell to her knees under the weight of his troubles, refusing to accept it, though powerless against it. She wished she could show him that she was all he ever needed.

"I can't believe this is happening," she said again. And again. And again. Each time with a slightly different tone and timbre. "I can't believe this is happening." She repeated these same six words at least a hundred times in a row, rocking back and forth on the floor, a mental patient's sway, knees tucked to her chest, a lifeless stare in her eyes, a look he'd never seen in her before. Each time she repeated it, it sounded different—angry, sad, helpless, manic—and yet each time she restated the obvious, it was exactly the same. "I can't believe this is happening."

Eventually she regained enough composure to stop uttering this phrase and she asked questions in an effort to keep their marriage from disintegrating right there in their diningroom.

Tears cascaded down her face and then his face, rippling against her sorrow, his guilt.

"How could you love me and not want to be with me? I just don't understand."

"One doesn't equal the other," he said and then paused for what felt like an hour. "I'm just not happy."

"How? I don't get it. I'm so happy when you're here. I'm happy *only* when you're here. I'm miserable without you. It sucks when you're gone."

It sucks when I'm gone. You're miserable without me. This was usually the point in their conversations where any meaningful dialogue would trail off, where the Troubled Man would terminate the exchange, thinking of ways he might be able to stay and be personally miserable but find ways to continue to mask his otherwise blatant despondency to make her happy, to hide his fear and anger and sadness to protect her from hers, to justify staying at the expense of his own happiness, his own sanity, so she could be happy, or honestly just so she wasn't sad, even though he knew that that wasn't what she wanted from him, that she didn't want him to stay if he didn't honestly want to stay, but she was lost because she wanted to find a way to make him stay, to make him *want* to stay, to make him realize that she could make him happy, that he could stay and get rid of his depression and sadness and anger, and that he didn't need to leave to be saved. But he was gone, so completely gone that there was nothing left, not a clinging breath of presence, and yet she felt something in her body try to hold him there. When she had first met him, his dreams were as heavy as cement. Eight years later, his dreams didn't seem to exist.

"So you want me to stay—you want me to stay even if I'm not happy?" He asked, half-rhetorically, half-hoping for an easy answer he hadn't thought of. But such an answer didn't exist; he knew this already, and he knew he had to go. She could keep his last name; he didn't care about that. She could keep everything. He just wanted to be free, just wanted some solace, just wanted to calm the clutter within.

"I want you to *want* to stay. I want you to be happy, Jody."

The Troubled Man didn't know how to respond, so he didn't.

She told the Troubled Man things he didn't want to hear, things he knew were true but couldn't change how he felt inside. She told him candidly that he would never be able to love anybody if he didn't first love himself. He knew she was right. She told him no one would ever love him like her. He knew she was right about that too. And the words that stung the most were her final words, her final plea, when she told him he would never be happy because he wouldn't allow himself to be happy. There was a huge lump in her throat that forced her to struggle for her words. She asked him why she deserved this. She yelled these words to keep from crying, and then she cried when she couldn't hold back the tears, lying on the kitchen floor, dry-heaving, hopelessness taking over her features, asking the air "Why?" and "How could this happen to me?" The truth was that this moment had been coming for a while. They both knew this, but people often avoid the truth for fear of destroying the illusions they've built.

The Troubled Man reached for the Kleenex box and handed her several sheets of tissue. He sat there, looked at her, and didn't know what else to do. They couldn't be nearer, yet they were a thousand miles away from each other. He thought of their time with one another as being lost together, as if he'd led them into a secluded forest, and they were lost because of him.

She had followed him to a place cut off from the rest of the world, and as long as she continued, she would be lost. The only way for her to be found was to stop following, to turn around now and leave him alone, leave him wandering beneath the darkness of the trees on his own. He knew something was going to continue to draw him toward the darkness and her only hope was to find a way out alone.

FIRE ENGINE RED

"Really? 'Go wash your dick and pee'—she actually said that?"

"I swear, Eric. Then she corrected herself like 'Wait, pee first. Then go wash it.'"

"What?"

"I know, right? She said she felt an itch and it might be like, you know—"

"What?"

"You know, like the first signs of a yeast infection or something."

"Gross."

"Nah. Not really."

"No, that's gross. Does she get around a lot?"

"I don't think so."

"Really?"

"What? What's that look for? I don't know. It's not like I asked her."

"Why not?"

"Well if I did ask her, then what? You think she's going to

be like, 'Yeah, I'm with all kinds of guys. You're like the eighth guy that's been inside me this month!'?"

"I dunno, maybe."

"No. She's going to be like 'Look at me: I'm young, I'm attractive, I'm tight down there, I take care of myself, and I don't sleep around.' And I'm going to look like a real asshole for even asking."

"I'd rather be an asshole than a nice guy with a yeast infection."

"Guys can't get yeast infections, dumbass."

"Whatever man. There's a million other things you can catch though."

"Nah, I'm clean. And anyway what about this whole double standard?"

"What double standard?"

"How come guys can have sex with all kinds of women and we're considered *manly* or whatever, but if a woman has more than one partner, she's a slut? That doesn't make any sense."

"Yes it does."

"How?"

"It's easy. It's all about the key and the lock."

"The key in the lock?"

"Yes. Keys *and* locks. Men have the keys, women have the locks."

"What are you talking about?"

"When you have a lock that accepts a bunch of keys, what do you have?"

"I don't know. What?"

"A lock that works with a bunch of different keys is a *broken lock*."

"OK."

"But when you have a key that works in multiple locks, what do you have?"

"A master key?"

"Exactly. A key that works in as many locks as possible is a *master key*. Broken locks and master keys: that's your answer."

"You're crazy. You know that right? Besides, women don't get yeast infections from having sex with a bunch of guys."

"Then how do they get one, Jody?"

"Hell if I know. Who do I look like, Dr. Phil?"

"You've got too much hair."

"Look. I'm just saying. We had sex a bunch of times and then she got a yeast infection."

"And *I'm* just saying you need to be careful. Just because you're divorced doesn't mean you can—"

"*Dissolution.* It's a dissolution, not a divorce."

"Same difference. And anyway, it doesn't mean you have a hall pass to stick it in anything that walks by."

"Yeah yeah yeah I know."

"Really?"

"What? I know, I know. Anyway, the day of the itch, she was like fire engine red, like down there. I mean like *red* red."

"What?"

"Yeah, she thinks it's from me going down on her."

"Wait. You went down on her?"

"Yeah and a day later she was … she was putting yogurt up in her. Like, up there, you know?"

"Up in her?"

"Yeah. Yogurt. Up there where the sun don't shine. Said she heard about it from from some medical website."

"Gross."

"It was kind of hot, honestly."

"You're messed up, Jody."

"I'm being serious. She's sexy as hell, irrespective of her predisposition for yeast infections."

"Is that your official diagnosis, doc?"

"Yes it is."

"Well I do agree with one thing though: she *is* smokin' hot. She always looked like she was on it."

"Yeah she's *on it* alright."

"Ha-ha."

"Oh and she asked me to piss on her. You know like—"

"Whoa whoa whoa. She asked you to *piss* on her? Like take your dick out and pee on her?"

"Yeah. No lie."

"Like in her mouth? She wanted to drink your piss?"

"No no no. That's disgusting. She, you know, she just … she just got in the bathtub and wanted me to pee on her. Said it turned her on."

"Bruh, that's crazy."

"I know. Freaked me out a little too."

"That shit would definitely freak me out. You didn't do it did you?"

"Hell yeah I did it."

"Ha-ha."

"What?"

"You're insane."

"Seriously though, it's totally cool between me and her. I don't think she's even sleeping with anyone else. She's totally into me. You should see the way she looks at me."

"That's cool, but chicks have always been into you. You just blocked it out for so long. Just be careful is all I'm saying. This chick seems a little crazy, a little slutty too. I bet she gets around."

"I hear you man. I will."

"Good. I'm going to get a refill on this. You want anything?"

"Yeah, sure. What was that girlie drink you had?"

"A soy latte."

"That's some gay shit."

"Whatever, prick."

"Just get me a large coffee."

"A *venti*?"

"Whatever."

THE WRECKAGE

Jody Grafton felt like a dreaded thing. Tax season. Rush-hour traffic. Sunday-morning church service. He was a burden—their burden—and for some reason they were compelled to accommodate him. He was simply another one of their obligatory chores, part of the minutiae of their day-to-day lives, the thing that was necessary to make everything else operate as it should.

The hospital is discharging me because
I no longer want to kill myself.
The social worker recommended
someone other than you pick me up.
I don't want to talk to you.

This was the long message Jody typed on his phone, but he didn't send it. Instead he attenuated the text to say only:

I wish I never met you.

But he didn't send that one either, and he felt like a coward for even typing it. Plus, he didn't want Jolene to call him after she received it. She was, after all, the reason he was sitting here in this hospital gown giving urine and blood samples and answering droves of questions from police officers and paramedics and administrators and nurses and doctors and even a social worker —an aloof, uncaring woman who spoke broken English.

The hospital smelled faintly of ammonia. The distant fragrance of lilac lingered beneath the chemical smell overwhelming this first-floor psych ward. The smells wafted into Room 33. A few monitors made the clicking and beeping sounds required of monitors at work. An out-of-sight patient down the hallway corridor shrieked something incoherent in a tone that seemed to sum up every feeling Jody felt at this moment. He sat up in the small bed and looked around his room. A switched-off TV was mounted on the wall opposite the bed. The white walls all around him said everything there was to say about loneliness. The room looked and felt cold. It *was* cold. Cold and sparse and sterile, but it could have been worse. At least it wasn't one of those padded rooms. At least this hospital gown wasn't a straight jacket. At least he didn't die from all those pills.

He looked up at the machines monitoring his existence. He wasn't sure how he was going to pay for all this. Was his life nothing more than a series of clicks and beeps and lines illuminated by red LED? He looked at the phone and erased the last text message. He called his best friend instead.

"Hello?" Eric, out of breath, answered on the fourth ring.

"I need you to pick me up."

"I'm kind of busy right now. What's up?"

"I'm at the hospital."

"What?" Eric's tone changed. "Where?"

"The new one right off the highway."

"Why?"

"I tried to kill myself."

A moment of wordlessness held the line.

"Shit. I'll be right there."

Jody thanked the ceiling and whatever gods were beyond it for friends like Eric.

A nurse brought him his clothes. His jeans and a bloodstained white teeshirt were wadded together, stuffed in a flimsy plastic bag alongside his sunglasses and wallet. It was the same bitch nurse who'd asked him for a urine sample earlier that day when he arrived at the psych ward after the ER doctors had pumped his stomach. He'd been too shaken up and too exhausted to urinate in the tiny cup she'd handed him. She told him she was going to get the sample with a catheter if he couldn't get it for her, to which Jody responded by locking himself in the bathroom until he was able to extract a little urine into the plastic cup and bring it back to Room 33.

"This ain't gonna be enough," she said, pondering the cup's half-inch of warm yellow liquid, holding it up and examining it in front of the room's hideous fluorescent lights. Her tone oozed annoyance. "If you can't squeeze out any more, we're gonna have to use the catheter," she reminded him.

Back in the bathroom, he tried to force the liquid from his bladder. Sometimes the easiest, most natural things are impossible to do under pressure. His black boxer briefs wrung around his right ankle, they dragged on the cold ceramic floor. He flung his paper-thin hospital gown over his left shoulder and tried vigorously to avoid a tube in his urethra. He shat on himself in the process, defecating mostly on the bathroom floor and on the back of the toilet, but he also felt feces running down the back of his left leg now, over the word MISTAKES tattooed to his calf, and down his ankle. Diarrhea of course. He'd never shat on himself before, not even while drunk, but immense stress does odd things to one's body.

A few hours earlier, before Room 33 and all the horrific lights and pitiful attention, he sat with Jolene inside his Chevy, parked with the engine running in a near-empty lot in front of Taco Bell. It was less than two months into the new year and every resolution had already failed. Jody took a long drag from his cigarette and looked out the windshield. He blew smoke at its already foggy glass and examined the Marlboro's tip like a lit fuse. He was going to quit these things one day, whenever he got around to it, New Year's resolutions and all. He gazed out the window through the haze. Jolene was yammering but he wasn't listening to her words as snow fell and covered every surface outside, even the blackened concrete and dirt around them appeared clean, a new beginning outside this fogged-up glass; a coat of fresh white absolved everything of its sins.

"You're not even listening, are you?"

"What?"

"I said you're not even listening, Jody." Her voice made him cringe.

"Yes I am."

"What'd I say then?"

He looked over and saw an outline of Jolene. He looked through her, not at her. That wretched feeling had returned in his stomach. He felt defeated, unbearably tired, as if she'd used up the best of him, and now she was scavenging through his remains. A few months ago, before the events of the last five months, Jody wouldn't've tolerated such pillory. He would have put any person—any man or woman—in his or her rightful place. But he didn't have it in him today. Plus he had just taken half a bottle of Ambien and everything was starting to go the way of the snow, a gradual fade to white.

Jody's mother, Irene, had passed five months earlier. Jolene came into the picture on accident, as his mother was dying and his marriage was falling apart, when everything felt upside down. He wasn't seeking it out. He hadn't wanted a new relationship. He didn't want much of anything at the time. If he did want anything, it was to stop the tailspin, and maybe Jolene could help.

Last August, Irene was moved from her home to a hospice end-of-life facility. She was thin and feeble with skinny, frail hands. Her pink scalp, fried from radiation, shone pitifully through her thin, white hair, what was left of it after the chemo. Jody visited her daily, clinging to a relationship they never had, attempting to recreate something that had never been created in the first place.

The hospice room was nice in a vapid, lifeless kind of way, mimetic of a motel's hollow decorations and creature comforts, which were supposed to make Irene feel at home until the cancer took her away. At times she smiled like the blind at a space where nobody was. All the hospice employees were nice, abnormally nice, especially a chipper young nurse named Jolene.

Jolene seemed to take better care of Irene than anyone else, including Irene herself. She snuck in special desserts from the cafeteria: chocolate mousse, key-lime pie, vanilla ice cream with peanutbutter on the side, whatever Irene wanted. Whenever Jody visited, Irene introduced the two of them with a hint of mischief in her eye. Her short-term memory was fading and she must have made that introduction forty times during her one-month stay, announcing each time that Jolene was single. Irene had never much cared for Jody's wife, though it wasn't apparent why. Each time Irene attempted to play matchmaker, he would smile at her scornfully and fiddle with the ring on his left hand, rotating it counterclockwise with his thumb contemplatively while glancing at Jolene and her embarrassed smile.

Irene was asleep almost every time Jody visited, her eyes closed and mouth open, breathing heavily, invoking childhood memories of her days passed out drunk on the couch, except now instead of empty bottles and cigarette butts, it was empty plastic dessert dishes that occupied the flat surfaces nearest her bed. Jolene gave overworked updates about Irene's condition: she was suffering as little as possible while under her care. They both avoided talk of the inevitable.

Jolene seemed so damn friendly every time Jody saw her. How was it possible to be this happy when you're surrounded by death? He started calling her "Jolly," sarcastically at first, but it stuck and Irene began using the nickname as well. Jolene played along. She enjoyed flirting with Jody and making Irene smile. She even changed her name tag to reflect her new moniker:

Dayton Hospice
Hello my name is
Jolly

As death approached, Irene hid from it in her sleep. Jody and Jolly would sometimes walk to the cafeteria and talk about Jolly's vague past and Jody's deteriorating present—anything to get their minds off the thing that was impossible to forget in this place. At twenty-seven she was a year younger than Jody, though she seemed infinitely more centered—*together* was the word Jody thought of when he thought of her. *She had it together* was a phrase his mother might have used. But Jolly was together only on the surface, a thick facade hiding something deep down. Over burnt hospital coffee, she told him about her life. Beneath her always-cheerful demeanor, Jody found a woman with broken parts inside. And so he listened to her tales of hidden sorrow and offered words of encouragement and listened some more and searched for ways to mend a heart he hadn't broken.

Near the end, Irene spent most of her time floating in and out of consciousness. A steady morphine drip eased the pain. Jody spent increasingly more time with Jolly while Irene rested, sleep before the final sleep, for which Irene and Jody both secretly yearned. Although they'd never acknowledge it aloud, they both craved an end to the suffering.

Irene told Jolly about her "famous" son's career as a singer-songwriter. And when Jolly mentioned this to Jody, she confessed that she had purchased all three of his albums in the last few weeks and that they remained on heavy rotation in her car's CD player. She told him she could relate to his lyrics and that she identified with the despair in his songs but also felt a sense of hope in his words, a sense of a brighter future, and it made him happy that she understood the emotions he felt while writing and recording those records. He told her about his touring days and his hapless dealings with his former record company and tried to explain why he stopped recording music nearly three years ago, but he wasn't completely sure why he had stopped and so he had trouble articulating his reasoning. Maybe he'd give it another shot one day. Maybe not. But he couldn't imagine doing anything else; he knew he couldn't possibly be anyone but himself.

A week-and-a-half into September, the summer weather cooled, the Ohio humidity diminished, and the leaves began to fall from the oak trees outside those sterile hospice walls. Jody and Jolly walked the manicured grounds as Irene catnapped. They knew she didn't have much time left, so Jolly showed up on her day off, wearing a summer dress that exposed her suntanned shoulders. She smelled nice and looked different without her scrubs. She could have been a model. The vernal September sun brought out a touch of blond in her hair and the white-tooth smile she showed off whenever Jody spoke.

They sat on a bench near one of the oak trees. They knew their time together would soon end. The temperature killed the summer days that had been keeping this alive, whatever *this* was. Under the shade of an oak tree, they said nothing; they just sat there and looked forward and wondered what was ahead.

"Shit!" Jody yelled.

Jolly broke her forward gaze and turned to him. It was shit. Literally. A bird had defecated on his shoulder. Jolly let out a hysterical laugh, a beautiful squeal of a giggle that made him laugh too; he couldn't help it. They both laughed and for that brief moment they were weightless together. It was time to face what they already knew. Mid-laugh, she leaned over and kissed him on the mouth, dead set on making this last. They both pulled away half-heartedly after a moment.

The following evening Irene went to sleep and she never woke. The evening sun through her window glowed rust red, and when it set, a thin pale pink hugged the atmosphere. The suffering had ended, at least for Irene. Jolly waited in the hallway next to the closed door. She cried while Jody sat in the chair nearest his mother and let his own tears stream down his face for the first time in his adult life. He gasped for air, sucking back the sobs, wiping away the unfamiliar wetness. *I'm sorry.* He apologized to Irene, said he was sorry that this life was so hard. He told her once more that he loved her and he prayed to any god that might be listening.

He went home with Jolly that night. Neatly folded clothes shrouded her second-story apartment: garments draped on chairs, on the sofa, on hangers—most surfaces swathed with her attire. She moved a stack of laundry from the couch, offered Jody a seat, and brought him a glass of water. He removed his sunglasses and tossed them on her coffeetable and drank half the water in one pull. Jolly comforted him with empty words. He leaned forward to set his half-empty glass on the coffeetable and as he did she reached over and rubbed his back lightly with her tiny hand. He looked over and wanted to kiss her, but he resisted and leaned back on the couch and placed his arm over his face to hold back the tears. A million thoughts stampeded his mind as he sat there in silence, completely lost in tumbling reverie. Ambient traffic on the nearby highway was the only noise. Thoughts toppled each other: thoughts of his mother, of his childhood, of his first guitar, of his brother and the events that took him away nearly a decade earlier; thoughts of his wife, Kelly, and of their wedding day, of their lapsed bliss which had expired early into the marriage. Why did he get married? And before he realized what was happening his dick was inside Jolly's mouth. Her wet tongue caressed his semi-hard shaft through his unzipped jeans. He hadn't moved, still leaned back, his arm covered his face. But he didn't try to move her either. He just reclined on the couch while the rush of thoughts dissipated. Eventually she came up for air and pulled the tie from her hair and long locks fell in her face. There was little light, just enough to see her features. She straddled his lap and then kissed him forcefully, passionately with intent. He returned her kisses without thought, a chemical reaction. Every motion felt hurried, hasty, urgent. She breathed hard, her sounds and breaths a healing melody. As they kissed, she forced his hand below her dress—panty-less and clean shaven and sopping wet. Everything was slippery. The sex that night was an awkward, violent blur. The couch. The wooden chair on the other side of the livingroom. The diningroom table. Atop the bathroom sink. The bedroom's carpeted floor in front of a full-length mirror. Her bed, eventually, tangled in the sheets. Angry and sad and intense lovemaking, enough sex and aggression to earn them Sigmund Freud's admiration. She was thin, much smaller than him, but he was the one who was breakable, fragile from a decade wrought into something blunt. They breathed heavily from too much thrusting, forceful intercourse in which tongues and fingers guided the way, a lover's Braille. It all happened in an instant, skydiving into the act itself, but it lasted into the morning. Her beautiful screams, her jungle of hair, her sweat on his skin. She orgasmed repeatedly that night, and so did he, until the sun rose somewhere outside the closed curtains. As Jody lay there post-coitally, uncertain of the next move, apocalyptic memories of the last year flooded back in. It was unfortunate that the painful emotions were always the ones that seemed to linger, while the pleasant ones vanished so quickly.

Jody left her apartment that morning after an hour of semiconscious sleep. That afternoon he drove his Chevy across the borders of sense and waded out into whiskey-and-water—brown bottles and mugs and shot glasses. He drank until he felt the floor shift, everything happening faster than it usually did; a cigarette seemed to last ten seconds. He drove home with beer on his breath and told Kelly he was leaving. He didn't explain why because he knew she would forgive him if he did; he knew she would convince him to stay.

He spent the next four months with Jolly, sleeping at her apartment. He had nowhere else to go. The first few months were great, an air of freshness, a feeling that both persons could do no wrong. They cooked dinners together and watched movies and had plenty of sex in exciting places and new positions. They stayed up late and talked. She asked questions that seemed innocent enough on the surface—*If you found the right person, would you ever want to get married again? Why don't you have any kids? Do you want to have kids someday? Are you going to get another record deal? How much money can a musician make?*—but those questions masked her real questions, questions that were meant to change him in some way, accusatory questions, condescending questions, belligerent questions to which a wrong answer could kick up a dust storm of fury within her reactions— *But how could you know for sure that you don't want to get married again? I bet you just need to find the right person to have kids with; that's the problem. I thought musicians made more money than that? You know, like all the rockstars and rappers you always see on TV?* —all of which he dismissed casually, because women are complex, insecure creatures. And so was he.

The following months brought with them the end of autumn, the fall that transformed happiness into unrest, the winter of discontent. Their hearts had bloomed and then faded against the chill. By January he stuck around only because he needed a place to stay. She hassled him daily, asking when was he going to stop drinking and stop smoking, and when was he going to make more music and get a new record deal, and when was he going to take her someplace warm for a few weeks, and when was he going to get the divorce papers signed?

When was she going to shut the fuck up?

But the first signs of real trouble surfaced one evening during dinner at an overpriced downtown restaurant (her pick), the kind of restaurant in which people pay for the "ambience" and patrons struggle to pronounce the foreign names of menu items and portion sizes are appreciably smaller than the portions at less-stuffy local diners. They sat across from each other beneath under-illuminated restaurant lights, a small table for two, talking and masticating, a lit candle on the table between them, a milieu of violin and cello in the soft air around them. Jody felt out of place in his jeans and untucked black button-down shirt, its top two buttons undone, exposing a small portion of a half-heart tattoo placed on the wrong side of his chest (i.e., the right side of his chest). Two children, a scurrying brother-and-sister duo, zig-zagged through the establishment. The boy, who looked a couple years older than his sis, accidentally ran into Jody's chair, tumbling onto his lap. He lay there awkwardly for a moment, staring up and laughing and smiling at Jody. The boy was wearing a polka-dot bow tie.

"Hey there, buddy." Jody patted him on the head. "I like your tie."

The embarrassed boy giggled and scrambled to his feet, spotting his sister who was frozen with excitement a few feet away. The boy made a silly half-roar and bolted toward his sister who let out a sharp, playful shriek, darting away in the opposite direction. Jody smiled and turned back to Jolly.

"You are so good with children," she said and smiled widely, a smile that was more suggestive than complimentary.

"Thanks. You know me, I'd make a great uncle. "

"Uncle?"

"That way I can give them back to their parents when I'm done being Cool Uncle Jody."

"Really? As good as you are with kids? I think you'd love them once you had a few."

"No, I don't think so. Never had the desire."

"That's so hard to believe," she said with exaggerated astonishment, a heavy heart beneath her fancy dress. "Can't you picture a couple of little rugrats with blond hair and blue eyes— just like you. You know we'd produce some great kids. Some smart, attractive kids." He knew she was right, but that didn't change his desire.

She asked him to please take the napkin out of his shirt and fold it over his lap, which he did begrudgingly while she continued talking about the prospect of children. He didn't like the way she was pushing the issue, and she didn't seem to like the way he resisted it. It was clear that she thought he was close-minded about the whole thing, not willing to see her obviously more rational side of the story. Who wouldn't want kids? He had fallen in love with her, hadn't he? She had certainly fallen in love with him, and all she wanted was for him to give her the babies and the lifestyle she deserved. And yes he did love her. But all he wanted was to be enough—enough for her. He wished she could be satisfied with him, only him, without needing all those other things, without wanting children or a suburban house or the fancy dinners he could hardly afford or any of the superfluous stuff outside the two of them. To him, *she* was enough. And yet somehow he could never be enough for her. Everything he had wasn't enough. All of him wasn't enough. Sometimes love itself isn't enough either. Or perhaps she was *too much* for him. He wasn't quite sure which. He wished he'd thought about all this before getting involved.

What Jolene wanted was everything she thought Jody could give her. In exchange she thought she could make him happy. She saw a man plagued with past sorrows—it was evident in his music, in his demeanor, in his actions—and if he couldn't fix what was broken, then maybe she could bring him joy. She thought that if she made him happy, he would change everything about himself. She thought she could emasculate him and somehow tame the beast. She knew she could, by means fair or foul, make him want kids and a house near a cul-de-sac with a dog and a yard and a fucking white picket fence and all the meaningless junk her yuppie parents fought about before they divorced a decade earlier. Somehow this would happen, even though, strangely, according to Jolly, these were also the reasons why Jody should leave his wife: *your goals just aren't aligned; you're not going to be happy if you stay; it's better for the both of you if you just end it so you can both move on with your lives;* and so forth. But it sounded like she was describing their own relationship, warning him that he should leave before it was too late. Yet it was impossible for him to deny his role in the whole thing, to deny that he'd perpetuated and complicated things with Jolly, but he was a Mozart of compartmentalization, grouping his own problems and separating them from the events at hand, so it was easy for him to ignore his role in all of it. Of course everything ends, the inevitable is always inevitable. Nevertheless, Jolly worked hard to change him, thinking he wouldn't mind the bother. She was blinded from the truth by the facade of her desires, so she stayed with him and ignored the obvious incongruities between both people. Something will change, she thought, although she didn't know what would change or even how they would begin to change it. Her love was only pain well-concealed. But in a perverse way Jody may have been secretly rooting for her. He wanted to change something inside himself and maybe she was the one who could facilitate his radical transformation.

Subsequent weeks led to subsequent arguments, intense arguments for which Jody didn't have the appetite, so they usually ended with Jolly's yelling or crying or both as he listened silently. Quietly wanting out of each argument, Jody fell into the cold caress of helplessness. He just wanted to return to the way things were right after his mother died.

And then, one day, he decided he had had enough, so he left and didn't return for several weeks. He lost contact with this world, finding other beds to sleep in, other women who wouldn't badger him or question him or give him a hard time, single women who had complex relationship issues and were looking for someone to fill the empty sides of their beds, married women who lusted for something else, something different, something they could never have, which he could provide them, a moment of satisfaction followed by a lifetime of subtle regret.

Jody turned off his phone during those weeks. He was unreachable—inaccessible—and he liked this feeling. He had been out in the open for so long—available, vulnerable, exposed. His music had perpetuated this. He had opened himself up to the world but closed himself off to his own self, made his life accessible to everyone but him. This had to change. And so he tried to change it in the bedrooms of other women. He moved through these bedrooms uneasily. One at a time, two bodies in a room. He hated who he was outside these rooms, but inside he was at his fundament—cold, mammalian, hard-hearted. He was pleased inside these rooms, pleased only in the moment though. Consequently, he never felt fulfilled, never felt satisfied with his life, a life of acting on impulse, a life without love, whatever that word was. He spent time looking into their eyes during the act itself, searching for something, a connection, a feeling of something more than what it was. Above all, he wanted them to love him, to need him in ways he didn't need them.

Jolly couldn't get a hold of him after the first two days, so she called Kelly. Neither woman had seen him in days and neither woman understood why they wanted to so badly—but they did. They both hung up the phone impolitely, directing their anger with the man they loved toward each other, or more accurately, toward their imagined versions of each other since neither woman had ever seen the other, not even a photograph of the other woman who loved the same man. Nevertheless, they shared one thing in common—they both saw something Jody didn't see in himself, the potential for a better man, the kindhearted man who didn't want to be what he was but who couldn't be anyone other than himself. It was him who he was, but they saw a better Jody, a better man who was caring and kind and even loving in his own way, not the cold, distant, manipulative man that lingered at his coarse facade.

Jody's life lacked a particular meaning. He looked around the motel room he'd occupied for the last three days after running out of beds to share. The TV was on, a window to a different world, an involuted world made shiny and new by the smiles on all the pretty faces. *Is this it? Is there nothing more?* The room itself reminded him of his mother's hospice room, which then reminded him of Jolly. He put on a teeshirt, grabbed his leather jacket and sunglasses, found his car keys, left the TV on, and drove to her apartment after two weeks without contact, not even a phone call. When she opened the door the look on her face said she wanted to smack him and hug him and kiss him and make love. She settled for three out of four.

Their bizarre make-up sex felt awkward, like driving a car through a shallow river: it didn't feel right but it worked and he got to the other side. And by the next day she acted like everything was back to normal, quickly back to the way things were: the same condescending questions, the same I'm-going-to-change-you attitude. But she wasn't going to change him, even though she desperately wanted to. She wanted to make him the man she wanted, and he wanted to be that man without changing. Things have a weird way of settling back into their natural form. Each sunset danced in the dust of another one of their days.

By February, Jody couldn't sleep. And when he did sleep, his nightmares haunted him. His relationship with Jolly peaked and valleyed that month, mostly valleys, so many valleys that all the peaks seemed to be behind them. The children thing came up quite a bit. He kept seeing her but got his own apartment close to the old neighborhood of a decade ago. The neighborhood was the same, but everything felt different. That old world was a lifetime ago—several lifetimes ago—and he didn't fit there anymore either. He didn't fit anywhere. The Ambien prescribed by the doctor at the clinic didn't help him sleep either; it simply diminished his consciousness, making his nightmares more nightmarish in their terrifying details. Hell on earth can be found in the subconscious.

Children poked their head into the conversation once again on the day of the incident. Jody walked into her apartment after having a smoke outside in the bitter cold. He took a seat next to her and explained as he had many times before that he assuredly didn't want kids, and that he was sorry but she would have to accept this fact and he wasn't willing to talk about it anymore and she shouldn't continue to try to change his mind—she shouldn't continue to try to change *him*.

For the first time a realization broke across her face, forming a palpable grimace. "You know what this means don't you?" she asked, in an almost rhetorical tone.

"Yes," he replied. If he didn't change, they couldn't be together. He knew this now. *They* knew this.

"What? I want you to say it," she said as her volume increased, angry and hurt, hovering near rage's ragged edge, a volcano of emotions waiting to erupt. "I want you to tell me *exactly* what it means."

"Why? We both know."

"I want you to say it. I want you to say that you would rather see me be with someone else—that you would rather see me *fuck* someone else—than have kids with me!" she yelled.

"You want me to say that? That's an odd thing to say," Jody said, deadpan.

"How can you be so calm and emotionless?"

"What? Do you want me to yell back at you? Do you want me to stoop to your level?"

"Stoop to my level?" she said and stood swiftly from the couch. "Stoop to *my* level? Fuck you, you heartless asshole!" she screamed, looking down at him.

"I don't know what to tell you. I don't want kids. Nothing you say or do is going to change that," he said, still seated. He was monotone and calm, which in hindsight he realized that maybe his flattened tone had gotten her that much closer to her boiling point.

"That's fucked up, Jody. You're fucked up! You've been stringing me along this entire time. Why? Just so you'd have a place to stay? Just so you'd have somebody to *fuck*?"

"No. Look, you're overreacting."

"You're such an asshole! You've been wasting my time all these months. How are you going to compensate me for my time? How will I ever get this time back?"

Compensate her for her time? It was time to leave before this whole thing got out of hand. He stood from the couch and attempted to remain calm by smiling at her grimly, an obvious mistake.

Darkness stole the light from her eyes. She didn't pretend to hold anything back. She let it out, let go of the frustration of the past few months, the frustration of an entire lifetime. Fuck. She punched Jody in the face. More accurately, she attacked him, hitting him repeatedly on his head and neck with closed fists. Jody couldn't believe what was happening. He'd been involved in a few fist fights in his lifetime, but he'd never been hit by a woman. Sure, he'd had his ass kicked before, and he could take a punch, but this felt different. For the first time in his life he felt defenseless, infantilized, completely helpless. He wished he could do something, but she kept swinging. A million puzzling thoughts came and went. *This bitch is crazy. What the hell am I supposed to do? How do I get her to stop?* His right ear rang from her haymaker left hook; the sound was deafening, but with his left ear he could still hear her scream the same three words over and over and over as she took wild closed-fisted roundhouse swings at him. The room shook under the weight of those three words.

"I hate you! I hate you! I hate you!" she must have said these words twenty or thirty times as he dodged most of her punches. She landed quite a few though, and she hit impressively hard for a hundred-pound girl. Those three words hurt much more than all the punches combined. But perhaps to hate someone this much you have to love them immensely. For a moment he understood how battered wives could repeatedly return to their husbands.

"Stop!" was all he remembered saying as he ducked and dodged not unlike boxer in the ring. A look of complete horror was his main reaction. He didn't know what else to say or how else to react. Everything moved in slow motion.

After what seemed like an hour but was probably more like forty-five seconds, she stopped swinging. "Hit me back you son of a bitch!" she said with hellfire in her eyes, showcasing that special kind of crazy produced by adrenaline and rage and wanting.

"No," he said, wincing, expecting another round of punches.

"Fuck you! You're totally fucked! I'm going to call the police and tell them you hit me. You're fucked!"

She yelled more, but he didn't yell back. It was pointless. Fighting back was futile. She was right—if she did call the police, he was in fact fucked. Everyone would believe her—a young, attractive, innocent-looking girl was hit by her tall, rough-looking, tattooed boyfriend. Of course they would believe her. Hell, he'd believe her. Which meant he'd go to jail and she'd have the upper hand. As long as they were together she'd always have the upper hand. She'd just proven she was capable of crazy, or maybe she'd proven she was in love, or perhaps those were the same thing.

She grabbed her phone and again threatened to call the cops. She screamed "You're fucked!" and "You're going to jail!" and similar declarations. It was time for him to leave. If she did call the police, he wanted to be long gone by the time they got there. He'd never had a positive interaction with the law. He circled the coffeetable and rushed down the stairs toward the entranceway, seeking safety outside these walls. Halfway down the stairs he felt a sharp pain on the back of his left arm and then a thud of something ricocheting off the wall and landing on the stairs behind him. He glanced over his left shoulder and saw a pair of pink-handled scissors with a six-inch blade several stairs above him. He grabbed his tricep; a runnel of blood trickled out where the scissors had penetrated his skin, a crimson stream ran down the back of his arm and over his tattoos; his own blood partially covered the word FREEDOM. Holding his teeshirt's sleeve over the small wound, he palmed his jacket from the coatrack near the door and stormed out of the apartment. The sun was high in the sky, dulled by winter clouds, and she was still yelling obscenities from atop the stairs on the other side of the door.

Driving and thinking, Jody searched for answers. He grabbed a stack of napkins from the Chevy's glovebox and bandaged his wound. Everyone bleeds, it's how we know we're alive.

He was tired. Tired of running from whatever he was running from. Tired of not having anything to run to. Tired of the sleepless nights. Tired of the nightmares that haunted him. Tired, just tired. The cars on the other side of the yellow lines sounded like waves crashing on the shore as they passed by. How long had his *check engine* light been illuminated? A long while, perhaps. So long that the problem was simply part of everything that worked now. He hadn't noticed it until this moment.

Jody pulled into a Taco Bell parking lot, ordered a burrito and a Pepsi at the drive-thru, and parked his car in front of the restaurant. Jolly called his phone eight times before he answered. He finally did answer, though he wasn't sure why. Sometimes he didn't understand his own actions. She sounded calmer, still shaken and tense but more composed. He told her where he was and that he was just getting something to eat and that he'd be back in a little while, although they both knew he wouldn't, at least not today. He hung up the phone and turned it off.

He finished his flavorless burrito, lit a cigarette and held it in front of his face—he stared at the fire in front of him. The car was parked with its engine running to keep the heater going. Through the rearview he could see inside the restaurant. A young girl—she couldn't've been older than twenty—sat at a booth near the window. He wondered about what kind of person she might be; he couldn't see her eyes. Two boys closer to her age stood next to her booth, flirting, acting as if they knew her. But it was obvious that they didn't know her, and Jody wanted nobody to know him too.

He finished his cigarette, tossed the burrito's empty wrapper on the floorboard, reclined his seat, and covered his eyes with his arm to maybe get some shuteye. Three minutes. Five. Eight. Ten. Glovebox. Ambien. Take two. After fifteen minutes he still didn't feel tired. He pulled the prescription bottle out of the glovebox again. The diaphanous orange plastic glowed against his fingertips. The bottle was half empty. Fuck it. He unscrewed the top and washed them down, all of them, with a few gulps of watered-down pop, and floated offfffffff. Acceptance.

It felt like he had just closed his eyes when he heard banging on the passenger-side window. Startled, he launched forward and knocked his head on the Chevy's roof. It was Jolly. She yelled something on the other side of the fogged glass. "Let me in," perhaps. But he hadn't let anyone in ever. Not really.

He unlocked the door and she sat on the bench seat beside him, the closeness of doomed cruisers on a sinking ship. Snow was falling outside, a few flakes were still on her, melting now, momentary blips of perfection fading once they touched her skin. Her hair was wet. She started in right away, ferocious words crafted to inflict maximum damage. He lit another cigarette and looked out the windshield. Jolly was yammering but he wasn't listening to her words. Snow covered every surface outside, a coat of fresh white, everything absolved of its sins.

"You're not even listening, are you? What the hell?"

"What?"

"I said you're not even listening, Jody." Her voice made him cringe.

"Yes I am."

"What did I say then?"

"You asked me when the divorce paperwork would be final, Jolene," he said in a commanding voice that told her to keep her volume down, a voice that also conveyed apathy. He didn't much care about her question, and he wanted her to know that he didn't care.

She put a stray lock of hair behind her ear, exposing her thin face, which was red from crying. She noticed how drowsy Jody looked, a different kind of tired, his head nodding lackadaisically, eyes glazed. It looked as though he couldn't keep his eyes open. Then she saw the prescription bottle on the floorboard and panicked.

"How many of these did you take?" She held the empty bottle in front of his face.

"None. That's an old bottle," he lied and leaned back in his seat. "I just need to get some rest."

She didn't believe him and so she dialed 911 and Jody leaned back and waited for whatever was going to happen to happen. He had no idea what to do, although he had a feeling it didn't matter. He hoped this would be the last time he saw her, in this snowy parking lot, her tiny hands gripping his belt buckle so he couldn't leave, waiting for the police to arrive, sheer panic in her eyes; her eyes confessed everything, a look that told him she was trying to hold on to much more than just his belt. He hoped that this was not the way he would remember her. There were good times after all, weren't there? He knew he would miss her; he would never get to say goodbye, never get to kiss her one last time. He would ache to hear her voice again, and it would be difficult to let her go. Love's treachery doesn't allow one to forget. It's hard to understand why we feel the way we feel. Not much made sense anymore: music, women, marriage, family. What did these words mean? Sometimes we have to get everything we ever wanted before we realize that everything we wanted is not what we wanted at all.

Two police cruisers barreled into the parking lot as if responding to a hostage situation. Two officers jumped out of their squad cars with tasers drawn. The ambulance arrived two minutes later and trucked a semiconscious Jody to the emergency room where they pumped his stomach and admitted him for standard-procedure psychiatric evaluation. When the doctor and social worker said he was allowed to leave the hospital, he called Eric.

It took Eric nearly an hour to get there, just enough time for the bitch nurse to bring Jody his wrinkled clothes, wadded and tossed in a small plastic bag. The bag was accompanied by a two-page list of "recommended" psychiatrists and psychologists, a 24-Hour Crisis Hotline refrigerator magnet, and a stack of forms to sign, which he signed without review. God only knows what he agreed to.

Eric drove them away from the bright lights of the hospital. There was silence. It was nighttime now, the day had lost its light, a white snow dusted the empty fields on both sides of the highway. The air felt crisper as the seasons prepared to changed. An entire world was in the sky in the rearview, clear and denim blue, hours from the vanished sunset.

"I knew she was crazy when you said she asked you to piss on her," Eric said. "Don't worry about it. I bet she was with other guys anyway."

Jody smiled and nodded; he slipped his sunglasses on and reclined in his seat. Although he was trying his best, Eric's words didn't make him feel better. The rest of their conversation didn't need to be had out loud. Eric already knew the story without Jody retelling it. Jody had hit rock bottom and they both knew it. But sometimes rock bottom is the finest place to be—the view can be astonishing.

As they drove north, Jody wondered what the future would hold. Maybe a stomach full of pills and a day in the hospital had broken his three-year spell. He had to move on. A man must fall before he can get back up.

Jolene called a few weeks later with unexpected news, news that forced Jody back into her life, whether he wanted it or not.

"Hello? Jody?"

There was an extended silence.

"Hello? Are you there?"

"Whadda you want?"

"What do I want? What do I want! What do you mean, what do I want?"

He did not speak. Silence held the line.

"I'm pregnant."

"Whaddah you talking about?"

JOSHUA FIELDS MILLBURN

"I. Am. Pregnant. Jesus Christ, Jody!"

"Bullshit."

"Bullshit? What do you mean, bullshit? What are you going to do about this, Jody?"

"Name that kid Houdini. I always wore protection with you."

"What? No you … You're such an asshole! I can't believe that you're just gonna—"

"Whoa, whoa, whoa. Stop all that yelling. Hey, listen, tell me something, Jolly."

"What?"

"What has a little dick and hangs upside down?"

"This isn't the time for some stupid joke."

"No, seriously, it's a serious question. What has a little dick and hangs upside down?"

"What the hell are you talking about, Jody?"

"A bat. It's a bat. A bat has a little dick and hangs upside down."

"What? Have you been drinking?"

"Now, what has a big dick and hangs up?"

Dear —— y,

I've been writing this letter every night in my head for weeks, every night as I lay there thinking of you, wondering whether you're alright, wondering what you're doing and what you're thinking, wondering whether you think about me even half as much as I think about you.

Each day, thoughts of you tumble through my head and my mind wanders through memories of us together. The good times: The first time I touched your hand. The first time we kissed. Your face illuminated by streetlights. The way we

147

looked at each other every time we made love. It felt different. Connected. It feels like it was yesterday, but yesterday is so far away.

And now everything feels OK these days . . . until I think about you. But you're always on my mind, even still. Every song on the radio is about you. When I'm driving, every car is your car — at least for a moment — and when I try to get a glimpse of you, the driver is never the person I hope to see. I walk past the places we used to go and I feel the warmth of you beside me. I see pictures of you, and I force myself to look away, otherwise I'd never stop staring. I hear your voice sometimes and I love it, and yet I hate it.

It's hard for me to spend time at home these days. I don't even want to be in this city. I see traces of you in everything. You are everywhere. And yet you are gone.

I still dream about you. I reach over for you at night, involuntarily, but you're never there and I always find an empty bed. And so I lie there and wonder whether you've already moved on, and if you have, are you happy with someone else? Do you light up the same way you used to light up with me, with that same look on your face? Do you miss my smell, my touch?

Sometimes I think I'd give anything just to hold you one more time, to sit with you on the porch, next to that silly little statue, just one more time, not even saying anything, just sitting there, next to me, together.

But I'm not writing this letter to get you back. I know that's not possible. I know that we're not possible and that we can't be together. I don't claim to have what you're looking for. But I also know that I love you, even now, even though we fell apart. And I know that I'm sorry for the way it ended. If I had it to do over,

I'd change the way it ended — I would somehow remove your anger and your hurt if I could — but I'd still love you the same way. Even if my love wasn't enough for you, or if it was too much. I'm sorry I wasn't what you required. You wanted more than I could be. You wanted more than Me, a Me who wasn't really Me.

Although you brought me some of the greatest joys of my life, you also carried with you the most excruciating pain I've ever experienced. Some of the things you did and said hurt me terribly, deeply — it was a particular kind of Hell for me — but there's no need to recount those things here. I don't think it was your intention to hurt me, but it hurt nonetheless. It's in the past now, and although I have a hard time forgiving people, I forgive you, even if you don't forgive me.

And I'm sorry I hurt you. It haunts me. I never meant to — I wouldn't ever want to hurt you. All I can do now is apologize. I'm sorry. I wanted you to be happy then — I swear I did — and I want you to be happy now and in the future without me. I'd rather you be happy with someone else than unhappy with me. I hope you find what you want, whatever you're looking for. Somewhere. I'm still on your side. I always have been.

I'm sorry, but this is the only way I know how to say goodbye.

Love,

— Y

PART THREE || **Alone Together**

SPEAKING OF OHIO

The day's breakneck pace of thoughts and emotions produced eight songs within four-and-a-half hours on that Brooklyn rooftop—Jody Grafton's first songs in over three years. He wrote the words *Lost Songs* on the front of his notebook. A new song started every few pages, each title scribbled in large, sloppy, capital letters at the top of each page: songs about his brother, his lost career and the perniciousness of the record industry, the passing of his mother, the last days of his marriage, the women he had taken advantage of, the loss of love, his problems with substance abuse, and his attempted suicide when he thought his life was no longer worth living. Each song was steeped in love and hate and the bottled emotions of the last decade.

Jody carefully descended the rusted fire escape and woke Michael so they wouldn't be late for their lunch with Michael's manager, Wes. Michael's eyes danced with confusion when Jody woke him, his short naps of hair clung to his scalp, unfazed by a night of deep sleep.

They sat across the table from Wes at a small, modern diner in Flatbush. Jody listened as Wes talked and Michael stabbed at his food like he was mad at it. The many shades of Brooklyn played through the diner's windows. Though they shared the same borough, the contrasts between this neighborhood and Michael's neighborhood were staggering. Flatbush looked like Bed-Stuy after fifteen years of gentrification. On this street alone there were trendy design businesses and coffeehouses and several florists with lavish window decorations and clothing stores with brightly dressed headless mannequins and various other new-age retailers. Unlike Bed-Stuy, none of these places were caged from the dangers of the neighborhood. Even the taverns appeared *au courant*. Flannel-clad hipsters peppered the landscape, and yet there was a bizarre diversity throughout the neighborhood, like something from a Harvard inclusion textbook. It was as if this neighborhood had its own EEO/AA policy: an Asian man and his black wife walked past the diner pushing a stroller with their cooing infant in tow; an ebony-and-ivory gay couple held hands and crossed the street at a nearby crosswalk, their trailing shadows tangled behind them; a prepubescent boy stood alone in front of a cupcake shop eating a chocolate chip cookie the size of his head, the flavors making a brown mess of his little fingers as he chewed and swallowed and made pleasurable sounds that most adults associated with intimacy; and a white lady in her late sixties carrying a paper bag filled with groceries was standing in front of a store, which in this neighborhood was called a "market" and back in Ohio was simply called a "store."

"It's like you just disappeared. What happened?" Wes asked while Jody observed the scene outside. Music-industry guys were always intrigued by stories of overnight stardom or by one's rapid plummet into oblivion. Jody's story contained both—twice the intrigue. It wasn't a case of *misery loves company*; rather, guys like Wes wanted to learn from others' successes and failures.

"Well," Jody looked up from his coffee. "That song came out when? Oh-six?" he tried to remember.

"Two thousand five," Michael jumped in. He looked excited, as though he wanted to tell the story for Jody and fastforward to the stories of the girls who came to their shows, though Jody was certain that their stories paled in comparison to any real rock tour. It wasn't like they had groupies slipping them hotel keys or throwing their panties on the stage, nor did they arrive back at their hotel (or motel, incidentally) rooms with four perfect-looking blondes with that I-want-to-fuck-you look on their faces. The truth of the matter was the fame felt electrifying, albeit short-lived, and they made some decent money, which they all probably wasted in a few months—it all went by so fast that it was hard to tell—and there were a few attractive girls who threw themselves at Jody, but he was successful in remaining faithful to his then-wife, though he realized a few years later that his tour-long abstinence was spurred by some sort of inner sanctimony, a self-righteousness, a morally superior high-road by which he traveled as a way to thumb his nose at the rest of the world. *Look at me, I'm so strong I can turn down women in every state.* And this act of Zen-like self-control made his band think that Jody Grafton was the coolest guy on earth, an image that stuck with them even years later.

"OK, oh-five. That song was on my second album, which came out about a year after my first. Yeah, that first album was mostly acoustic and it didn't sell too well but the label made its money back and so they decided to take their option for a second and third album."

"What label were you on? Universal?" Wes guessed, naming the largest record company in the world.

"Sort of. It was Geffen Records, who had been purchased several years prior—I think in the nineties—by Universal and folded into one of their imprints called Interscope Records."

"Ah, yes. Interscope: the former home of Death Row Records." Wes said in jest.

Jody laughed at the thought of being associated with Tupac Shakur and Dr. Dre. "Yes but Geffen basically handled the, ahem, *non-urban* artists for Interscope, which I'm pretty sure is the P.C. way to say 'white guys,' right?"

"Yeah. Guess that gives a whole new definition to the term *white label*," Wes said. "So how did you get a record deal with Geffen? That was a pretty big accomplishment, right?"

"Huge. But it's not like I just went straight to Geffen after playing a few local bars in Dayton. It took an excruciatingly long time to get anywhere in the music business."

Wes and Michael both listened, waiting for some kind of music-business secret as if a Zen master were explaining how to obtain a record deal.

"Let's see. I played a bunch of terrible shows for like three years after high school, from like nineteen to twenty-one. Well actually right out of high school I was involved in some things I shouldn't've been involved in and I almost went to prison, but that's an entirely different story for another day. And but then I played a bunch of gigs for like three years. You know, small clubs and bars in the Midwest, sort of perfecting my craft. Then I met my former manager, Joe, and he got me an indie record deal with this small label called Planet Records in Cincinnati right after I turned twenty-two. So that was like two thousand three I guess. Yeah and in like eight months, sometime in early oh-four, Planet Records went out of business, just folded up shop and I haven't seen the owner since. Someone told me he got busted for selling drugs but I'm not entirely sure what happened. So anyway they went out of business but not before I recorded an entire album worth of songs. Then my manager—who turned out to be a genuine asshole, a shady sonofabitch who essentially tried to steal all my publishing rights—he shopped that album around to a bunch of different record labels. And then Geffen had this new A&R guy, a guy named Brett Barker, who really loved my album. Brett was like this really cool bearded New York hipster-crowd guy—not a hipster himself, per se, he was too cool for that, but then of course all hipsters are too cool to be hipsters, that's why they're hipsters—but he was covered in tattoos and always wore black teeshirts and was probably working in a coffee shop like two weeks before Geffen hired him, but he was at the right place at the right time and he really loved my music. I mean like really, really loved it and believed in it and believed in me as a musician and made me believe there was still something good about making music for a record company, and he made Geffen believe there was like something magical about my music. He told them it was like Bruce Springsteen had made an acoustic album with Paul McCartney or some nonsense, which not only seemed grossly inaccurate and kind of stupid to me, but I remember thinking he was going to get laughed at for making such ridiculous claims."

"What did they tell him?" Wes asked.

"They told him to sign me. Immediately." Jody said with a surprised tone. "They saw how passionate this cool young guy was and they were like 'Hell, if this hipster likes this flavor of shit, then all the other bearded black teeshirts will like this flavor of shit too.' So they signed me to a one-album deal with a two-album option."

"Nice. It sounds like he honestly loved your music," Wes said.

"Without a doubt. I'm telling you, the first time my manager took me to meet Brett at the Geffen offices, Brett popped my CD in the stereo and started singing along with it. He'd had the CD for less than a week and he already knew the songs. I was blown away. It was the first time I'd met someone I didn't know and they already knew my songs. It was a little surreal. But it was exciting too."

"Amazing how the stars aligned. Then what?"

"Geffen changed the track order and then mastered and released that first album, *Into the Storm*. It basically cost them nothing to put out. I remember they didn't promote it very well, I think because Interscope kept a tight lid on Universal's coin purse, saving most of Geffen's promotional budget for proven acts or to fund its own hype machine for its hip-hop artists. But that's just my hunch."

"Sounds like you know how it works." Wes nodded to acknowledge the accuracy of Jody's hunch.

"Maybe. But I'm just guessing. I don't know about anything that happened behind the scenes," Jody said. "So anyway the album sold OK, even without the hype, or at least enough for Geffen to make a little money and pay me some scraps."

"Did you tour at all with the first album?"

"Oh yeah. I toured a lot in oh-four after the album came out. I had to: it was the only way to make any money. I did a bunch of acoustic sets, opening for a bunch of bands throughout the Midwest and the East Coast. Just me and a guitar in a car on the open road, which was kind of hard because I had just gotten married around the time I got signed and instead of playing a bunch of local gigs, which Kelly, my wife, was used to, I was now gone for like days or even weeks at a time."

"I bet that was difficult."

"It took its toll. I wrote a song about it for my second album, a song called "Sending My Love from Iowa City," which was supposed to be a sort of apology for being gone all the time, but my wife didn't see it that way. She saw it as an oblique way for me to justify my weeks of absence as if it was OK because I wrote a song about it. And you know what, she was probably right. It was all very complicated."

"So *Into the Storm* sold enough for Geffen to exercise their option for a second album?" Wes asked, probing the story along.

"Yeah. I had written half of the second album before I got signed by Geffen, and I wrote the other half while on the road and most of that half was about how I missed my wife, or rather how I *should* miss my wife, even though I'm not sure whether I really did." Jody paused for a minute, took a sip of coffee. "Anyway, I named the album *Out of the Storm*, which seemed appropriate at the time, like everything was looking up, like the storm was clearing and I had a prolific music career ahead of me and I was going to find a way to make the marriage work once I got off the road," Jody said, a twinge of sadness in his voice.

"And that was the big hit album? The one with that one song, right?" Wes asked, searching for the name of Jody's hit single, which showed the almost minuscule, limited success it actually had—it wasn't as though it was memorable like "Purple Rain" or "Hotel California"; it was a short-lived thing that made its way onto the radio for a few months, but that was all.

"Not at first. It was a slow burn to start. That album came out in the spring of oh-five. Geffen released the first single, 'I Won't Be There When You're Alone,' which I liked but I didn't think it was a single at all, let alone the album's first single, and it didn't get much radio play and so the label released the second single, 'Forgive Me,' in the summer, which I thought was the best song on the album and should have been the lead single, but of course that song got even *less* radio play than the first," Jody said.

"Really? Why?" Wes asked.

"No idea. Shows how much I know about picking songs I guess. A few college radio stations played it, but that was it. Maybe some Internet radio stations did too, but iTunes and all that Internet stuff just wasn't as big as it is today—this was right before that. And so I thought that was it, and it was all winding down now; I was on my fourteenth minute of pseudo-fame, just staring at the clock, waiting for that last minute to tick away. And then something unexpected happened. Those college stations who liked the second single started playing a song called 'Ohio Again,' which was—"

"*Ohio Again!* That's it! I've been sitting here trying to remember the name of that damn song. 'Ohio Again.' I knew I knew the song though."

"That's the one," Jody said, knowing that this song might end up being to him what "Never Gonna Give You Up" had been to Rick Astley, which seemed like an uncomfortably accurate analogy for his career, like Jody had Rickroll'd himself. He just couldn't see himself singing that song twenty years from now to a bunch of reminiscing middle-aged Gen-Xers with pleated pants, beer-bellies, and diverse stock portfolios. Just the thought of it made him question the meaning of life.

"Did you know that a bunch of college DJ's in New York

were sampling the piano from that song and looping the line you sang about New York?" Wes asked.

"Yeah, I heard about it, like all these New York DJ's were using the song in various ways, but no I haven't really heard any of the records that sampled it."

"It's true. It was massive for a second that winter."

"Did you know that Michael here is the one who convinced me to put that song on the album? He even played the piano part and sang the backup vocals on the last chorus. In fact I think that's why he wanted it on the album. So we crammed it on there at the last minute, placing it at the very end of the album. Track twelve."

"Michael did the chorus?"

"Yep. You know the part at the end that sounds like a giant choir? That's Michael recorded over himself like sixty times. Made it sound like a crazy crowd singing in unison."

"That's right, I'm the man behind the curtain—the real reason why Jody's rich and famous." Michael said in an almost earnest tone.

"Thanks but I'm afraid I'm not much of either. I'll happily give you credit for whatever short-lived success I did have though." Jody said, and Michael furrowed his brow. "Oh cheer up, Mikey, it was fun while it lasted."

"It was everywhere on the college radio stations around here," Wes said.

"I was shocked when it got a lot of play. It's very ironic though. That long piano part at the end—the part all the DJs were looping—that was supposed to be where the third verse went, but I never wrote one. It's funny how things work out sometimes: sometimes we're praised for the mistakes we make. I wrote that song toward the end of my senior year in high school

—literally *in fucking high school*—about a girl I'd been dating for like two years and she suddenly decided she was going to leave Ohio and go to college in New York and she said we should break up or have some time apart and but then she kept coming back to me and as a lonely high-school kid it felt like she was just playing with my heart. And yes I'm aware that that sounds extraordinarily cliche or melodramatic or whatever, but that's where the New York line came from in the song: *New York is where you want to be*."

"Yeah, that's the one they sampled over and over. Some pretty good mix-tape songs—*hip-hop* songs—were manufactured around that line. Some pretty bad ones too, but still, it was a crossover kind of song," Wes said.

"I guess so, in a weird way it was a crossover song. Though I never thought I'd be responsible for a sort of hip-hop anthem," Jody said. "So anyway, that song grew legs at the very end of oh-five, between Thanksgiving and Christmas, and I think the record company was just as shocked as I was. But they sent it out to all the Top 40 stations and paid all the DJ's and program directors to play the song and by the end of January the record company was helping me set up a headlining tour. Within a week Geffen went from wanting to drop me from the label to giving me a *per diem* account for tour expenses."

"Must have been exciting," Wes said.

"It was. I remember being excited but also unbelievably scared. But of course I tried not to let the fear show. Geffen wanted me to do this tour in like twenty-five or thirty cities across the U.S., but I had this grandiose idea of performing in one city in every state in the country, plus all thirteen provinces and territories in Canada, as well as a show in Mexico City and a small European leg of the tour in like five cities—London, Paris,

Barcelona, Rome, and somewhere else that didn't speak our language."

"Munich," Michael added. "Those German girls were amazing."

"That's right, Munich," Jody agreed. "So like sixty-nine tour dates."

"Sixty-nine?"

"Yes, although the euphemism was totally coincidental. Geffen thought I was crazy—and they ended up being right in the long run—but somehow Brett convinced them I was the one who sent 'Ohio Again' to the college stations—he never actually asked me about it and so I think he thought it was true. Or at least he *wanted* it to be true—you know, plausible deniability—but then again he always gave me way too much credit for things because he liked my music. And so Brett convinced Geffen that my idea of "leaking" the third single—'leaking' seems like such a bad-boy, antiestablishment term, I know—anyway, he convinced them it was brilliant and thus my tour idea just *had* to be brilliant too and they could use the 'every state' angle to promote the tour. And so they agreed to fund the tour after various rounds of arm twisting. They officially called it the 69 States Tour. But we soon dubbed it the Speaking of Ohio Tour, at least within our inner circle, because that was pretty much the only song most people knew at the shows: between songs at the shows people would yell out 'Ohio!' but we always saved that song for last. And on stage I would say smart-ass things like 'Speaking of Ohio, here's another song you've probably never heard,' and I would do that like four or five times a night, and by the time we actually got to the song the entire crowd was essentially begging for it, which I remember at the time being a major shot of adrenaline."

"Tell him about the girls," Michael said eagerly.

"I'll let *you* tell him. I got *none* on that tour. Nothin'. But I think you and Eric and Evan got more than enough to supplement my celibacy," Jody said.

"Wait. You were on a national tour with your name on the marquee in every state in the country and you didn't get any ass? You expect me to believe that?" Wes asked.

"Believe what you want, but it's the cold truth," Jody responded with a nonchalant air about him, like it truly didn't matter what Wes believed because only the truth mattered, when in reality it was the truth, but it was the truth only so he could tell people it was the truth, so they would hold him in some kind of high regard as a man with superior morals or values or inner-conviction, none of which Jody really possessed if other people didn't believe him.

"Oh it's true alright," Michael came to the rescue. "Jody is the most selfless person I know. He didn't even *look* at a piece of ass while we were on the road, but he made sure we were all taken care of, if you know what I'm saying?"

"You give me too much credit, Mikey."

"I've got to hand it to you, Jody. You're a stronger man than me," Wes acknowledged by almost bowing his head in respect, from which Jody gained great pleasure but simply waved off the compliment with a head nod that said he did what any man would do in his situation and there was nothing extraordinary about it at all.

"Anyhow, so the tour lasted most of oh-six, and it was a disaster for the most part," Jody said.

"A disaster?" Wes asked.

"Yeah. It turned out that my one-city-in-every-state idea wasn't such a great idea. It was great at first, but that's because we started on the East Coast. So the shows in like Boston and Philly and obviously New York were huge with like two thousand people, and we felt like the rest the tour was going to be the same way. But then we hit cities like Bangor, Maine and like Burlington, Vermont and places like that, and it was a dash of cold water. Plus we missed out in some other big cities and college towns in the states we had already been to, like Pittsburgh and San Francisco and Austin and a bunch of other cities that we skipped because we were doing just one city in each state."

"Not many people showed up at some of the smaller shows?"

Jody laughed. "I think our worst turnout was in Billings, Montana. I think eight people showed up, all guys, and four of them were there to see the opening act and left before we took the stage, leaving us with four guys at our concert, and all four of them had driven together to get there, so at first it seemed worse than playing in some Midwestern bar because we had these people's full attention and they still expected a full show, even though the audience-to-performer ratio was like one-to-one."

"Did you cancel the show?" Wes asked.

"Hell no, those college guys drove like four or five hours from Missoula, through like cow pastures or whatever, to get to Billings so we played as if there was four thousand people there. Strangely, I remember it being one of the most positive experiences of the tour. We went out with them afterward and they were real cool."

"That show was kind of lame though. Plus there were no girls." Michael said to Wes in an audible whisper.

"Maybe. But I enjoyed it," Jody said as if that was the final verdict and no other words could be used to more accurately describe their tour stop in Montana. Jody's sense of satisfaction from the small things irked Michael a bit but made him respect Jody even more, and Jody knew this.

"We ended the tour in Europe, playing to some small crowds, like one or two hundred people at each show who had heard the song on the Internet. We didn't think those cities would produce much of an audience, but we wanted to do it as sort of a vacation. The closest any of us had ever been to Europe was London, Ohio."

"Did you make any money from those European tour dates?" Wes asked, likely wondering whether it was possible for any of his artists in the future.

"We made a little money off of CDs and teeshirts at the merch booth, but the record company actually lost money, and they weren't too happy about it. They kind of felt like they were duped into paying for four guys to go sight seeing in Europe for a couple of weeks. Which, in all honesty, they kind of were."

"And Mexico?"

"It was anticlimactic. Let's see: we did the states first, heading from the East Coast to the Midwest to the South and then out West. And then we did thirteen shows in Canada from west to east, which weren't too bad. Vancouver was especially memorable; the most amazing people live in Vancouver. We went home for a few weeks to recover and then the record company flew us down to Mexico City. But the show got canceled because there was a bomb threat at the hotel that was attached to the venue where we were supposed to play. We sold only like maybe a hundred tickets, if that, but since the show was canceled, we just roamed the streets of Mexico City for two days before flying back to Ohio and then Europe and then finally back to Ohio again. The whole tour ended in like October of oh-six. And that was literally the last show I ever played—a small crowd of Krauts in Munich."

"But I thought you did another album after that?"

"Oh I did. Geffen was eager to capitalize on the success of the album; by the time we got back to the States it had gone gold, which I remember being this unbelievably shocking thing for me, like something I never expected, and I didn't know how to react. So they asked me to get to work on a new album that fall, which I was happy to do, because it meant I could spend some time alone and just think and reflect on everything that had happened over the last year, reflect on all the supposed success and try to figure out whether I was happy or satisfied with it. Plus I always preferred writing songs to singing them in front of people. There was something about the act of sitting in a room with a pen and a piece of paper and a guitar, just staring at a wall. It was the only thing that felt *real* to me. Sitting in the chair alone seems to be the only way to quench my thirst for solitude.

"And so I wrote the third album in less than a month and recorded it in a week right after Christmas at the beginning of 2007. My idea was to strip everything down to basically just me and a guitar and I had Michael play the piano and light percussion on a few songs but that was it. We even recorded it in this rundown studio, like in the backroom of a record store in Dayton. Just me and a guitar and a microphone—and Michael when I needed him. I turned in the album to Geffen right away, many of the songs I recorded on the first take."

"What did they say? Were they expecting something different? Something more *produced* perhaps?" Wes asked.

"No. Brett loved the album. *Loved* it. It felt right. Out of anything I've ever recorded, that album is what I'm most proud of. It wasn't perfect, but it was the best album I could've created at the time. Musically, lyrically, its continuity—it all came together on that album."

"The table was set for another hit record."

"Well, the buzz from 'Ohio Again' had died down significantly, although it was still the only song anyone talked about if they talked about me at all. So I borrowed our fake tour name and called the album *Speaking of Ohio*. But a week after I turned in the album, Universal, Geffen, and Interscope were rearranging the deck chairs, and there was talk of Geffen splitting off from Interscope and becoming their own imprint under Universal because they had been so successful with several hit records over the last couple years. But those rumors were quickly quashed when Universal decided to further fold Geffen into Interscope, laying off six Geffen employees in the process. And guess who one of those employees was."

"Not your A&R guy?" Wes said with condolence.

"Yep. They let Brett go. Hell, I can still remember the exact date: January 18, 2007. The day everything changed."

"Didn't they give you another A&R guy? I mean, you had already had a hit record and this album was ready to go, right?"

"Yes, they gave me another A&R guy. Some suit from Interscope. This forty-something chubby guy who had signed a bunch of overly synthesized poppy R&B acts on the Interscope side, and now he had similar ideas for Geffen. He wasn't interested in music; he was interested in assembling boy bands."

"He actually said that? He used the term 'boy band'?" Wes asked with a look that seemed to either sympathize with Jody or apologize on behalf of the entire music industry.

"Yes. He said he was looking for the next Backstreet Boys or whatever. He was swinging for the fences, which meant my record—which sounded more like a demo to him than one of his heavily produced bubblegum albums—was not a priority. I doubt he even listened to the whole thing."

"Did they still put it out?"

"Barely. They put out like a drunk girl at three a.m. Sloppy and tentative, without focus, something you regret doing in the aftermath," Jody said. "I remember the first week's sales were OK from real fans buying the album, but after the first week, sales fell of a cliff. Other than a few posters, they didn't promote the damn thing. They didn't even really make an attempt to sell the album. No radio. No TV. No Internet promotions. Nothing. If it sold, then it would be free money for Interscope, but if it didn't then they weren't out any money. So I just threw up my hands and bowed out. It wasn't a game I could win."

"And, *bam!* just like that, that was the end of your contract?"

"That was it. Three and done. I haven't written a song since —well, not until this morning actually. I didn't even do a single show for the third album. I was so livid with the record company that I just stayed in Ohio, and I remember drinking too much and not much else, and when my wife couldn't take the drinking anymore and she complained about it, I acted pathetically: I started yelling and being an asshole and then eventually the pendulum swung the other way and I just stopped talking altogether, sort of withdrew from life, and it was like we didn't know each other anymore, Kelly and I. Like we said goodbye without actually saying goodbye."

"Damn," Wes said with empathy.

"You know, I still hear 'Ohio Again' every once in a while and half the time I have this strange visceral reaction to it. Not to the song necessarily, but it's like looking back at a mountain you just descended from and now you're in the valley just looking up at the mountain and you're like, hmm, now what?"

"Well maybe that's a good question," Wes said as if he'd found a profound truth. "Now what?"

"I don't know man. Because the other half of the time when I hear that song, I love it for its serendipity. It's beautiful to think I created something in high school that resonates with people today. And it's beautiful to know that we don't really have any control over what happens, whether it's a song we write or a job we take or your high school girlfriend dumps you. You never know which tragic situation might actually turn out to be overwhelmingly positive."

"I guess you can thank the girl who broke your heart back in high school for that lesson then?" Wes said.

"Yeah. It's funny how things work, isn't it? I thought my life was over at seventeen. I mean, I thought she was *the one*, you know? But in a weird way she *was* the one. I mean, she was the one who made me write a song that a lot of people really liked almost a decade after writing it. Although at the time I just remember being sad and lonely, mainly because she kept coming back to me and then breaking it off and then coming back to me, and it was all very—"

Michael, in an attempt to lighten the mood, butted in to sing "Ohio Again's" chorus: "*You just stay the same / never making any sense / You come running back to me / over and over again.*"

And then Wes joined in. Everyone who had heard the song just once knew its simple chorus. It lifted Jody's spirits instantly, taking him back to the rush of the stage four years prior, the rush of the fans singing along and repeating the chorus over and over while he held his microphone in their direction.

You just stay the same / never making any sense / You come running back to me / over and over again.

It still felt like it did back then, even with two guys somewhat sarcastically singing it with the scorching sun beaming down on the streets of Brooklyn outside the window. And for the first time in years he felt the same kind of alive he felt back then.

NEW YORK IS WHERE YOU WANT TO BE

"How many people are out there, Mikey?"

"It's dark. It's kinda hard to see."

"Move over for a sec. Let me take a look."

"There must be like two thousand people out there."

"Crazy, right? I've never played in front of a crowd even close to this size."

"Eric, Jody, come take a look at this. Y'all'ren't gonna believe this."

"This place is packed! When we pulled up and that huge line was out front I thought we were screwed. I thought that line was like for some big event or something and it was going to block the people who wanted to come to our show. Hey, Evan, take a look at this."

"You sure they're all here for us?"

"No, numbnuts, they're here to watch *CATS* the musical."

"Actually, I think they're here to see *Jody*. Not us."

"Shut up. They're here to see *us*."

"That sign out front has only one name on it."

"Whatever. We're going to tear this place down tonight. You ready?"

"There's going to be a gang of pussy out there after the show."

THE SUMMIT

The Record Executive slouched moderately in his black high-back executive leather chair. The windows behind him displayed an impressive view of New York City, a view he paid little attention to other than the occasional glance, which didn't last more than a few seconds because men in his position don't have time to contemplate the cityscape. The title embossed on the gold nameplate atop his large mahogany desk read *Sr. Vice President Artist & Repertoire*. His office's walls were not adorned with his bachelor's or master's degrees, both of which he had earned two decades earlier, but instead contained the gold and platinum records for which he was responsible—seventeen in total. Beneath the framed records sat a dark, solid wood bookshelf with book titles such as *The Music Business Is a Competition* and *How to Quickly Eliminate the Opposition*, and there were more than a dozen pictures of him accepting various awards at a variety of industry events and framed newspaper articles featuring interviews of him discussing his record company's rapid growth since he took the reins of its A&R

department in the middle of the last decade (as well as the reins of several other A&R departments at a number of other record labels acquired in multiple merger and acquisition deals) and on his bookcase's bottom shelf stood two framed photos of his four children, to which he had court-granted visitation rights on Wednesdays and every other weekend. It's lonely at the top, he sometimes thought.

The Record Executive no longer had time to care for his health. The weight of his ex-athlete's body creaked the hinges of his high-priced chair's handmade mechanics. Over the years he had transformed into a doughy version of his former self, his jock-like strut displaced by a subtle limp, perhaps from the early stages of gout, his once thin frame supplanted by a man who weighed nearly twice what he had at the end of high school, his jowl drooping over his ever-tightening Brooks Brothers collar. Empty potato-chip bags and soda cans occupied the trashcan underneath his desk. He was less angry when he ate.

The Record Executive was ruthless in business meetings, though perhaps *ruthless* was an understatement. He yelled and screamed and elicited fear from the people around him. He knew exactly what he wanted and was willing to do whatever it took to make it happen. People who stood in his way were the opposition and of course he knew *how to quickly eliminate the opposition*. He had fired dozens of people over the years—it felt satisfying in the most primal of ways to throw his weight around like this, to terminate the weak, including a good deal of recording artists with successful careers (though not successful enough to meet his multi-platinum standards, often invoking one of his favorite platitudes as justification for ruining someone's career/life: "No singles or doubles around here. I'm only swinging for the fences!"). Survival of the fittest. People for whom he had no use were essentially dead to him; they did not exist.

The Record Executive was a brilliant man, especially when it came to business acumen and the acquisition of power and the art of competition. He was the master of manipulation. He knew how to get results and how to impress his bosses and how to impress his bosses' bosses and was willing to do things many people wouldn't even dream of doing to get those results. He was incredibly successful—at least ostensibly. He drove a luxury car, wore expensive tailored clothes, choked down large premium cuts of medium-rare steaks at swanky downtown restaurants, and brought home more money than anyone from his high school's graduating class, over ten times more than his blue-collar father brought home when the Record Executive was growing up in their lower-middle-class neighborhood to which he swore he would never return.

But everyone hated the Record Executive. His ex-wife loathed the mere sight of the man. Her new boyfriend—a man who was far more attractive than the Record Executive, and who was good to the Record Executive's ex-wife in myriad ways, treating her kindly and handling her and her kids with respect, making passionate love to her in what she considered to be a considerate way, always caring about her feelings and her satisfaction and whether or not she came several times before he even thought about experiencing the same pleasure—this man also despised the Record Executive. He detested him by proxy, even though he barely even knew the man, other than what the Record Executive's ex-wife had told him, often in a spell of post-visit or post-telephone-conversation anger.

The Record Executive's staff avoided contact with him at all costs; they took massive, often irrational, precautions to avoid personal contact with him whenever possible. Even the people he trusted most—the (exclusively white) men he considered to be part of his elite inner circle—they hated his fucking guts. It was a complex hatred that made the haters ashamed for their hatred and thus made them hate the Record Executive even more. They had twisted fantasies about him that they were ashamed to admit, fantasies like the one in which one employee—a twenty-something low-level A&R guy named Brett Something, whom the Record Executive had recently terminated as part of a merger —this young man imagined a rainy night after work in which the Record Executive could hardly see through the gelatinous downpour while a semi-trailer truck didn't notice his approaching luxury sedan and not being able to see the double yellow line in the middle of the road the Record Executive inadvertently veered left of center just enough to get clipped by the oncoming semi which caused his car to ricochet like a pinball off the semi's front end and smash through a guardrail causing him to plummet to a slow, painful, fiery death. Actually, more than one person envisioned a similarly dark fantasy. The smart employees learned to placate him if they wanted to sidestep his wrath. The Record Executive's ego forced him to like these yes-men even though he was more than smart enough to realize that they were only yes-men and they were simply agreeing with him for the sake of agreeing with him. But he loved their fear; it fed his deepest insecurities, of which there were many. He was terrified of being broke and unloved and, most of all, alone. It's lonely at the top, he often thought.

Deep down the Record Executive was completely alone and he knew this. He thought about it daily. He maneuvered with spiritual bankruptcy, seeking small deposits of pleasure and distraction, stalking the sea of cubicle farms each morning, badgering the bottom-feeders. He was emotionally broke and vastly unloved and utterly and empathically alone. After his divorce a few years earlier, not only did he lose his family, but he also lost his big house next to the fancy golf course and a huge chunk of his savings and much of his future income in the form of alimony, by which he had been—and still was—very frustrated, because he had no power over the situation. In love, and in its loss, he was a powerful control freak without control. Friends from the old neighborhood—the one with the fancy golf course—stopped talking to him after the divorce, perhaps after the stories of verbal abuse they had heard from his ex-wife, he thought, not knowing the real reason they stopped talking to him was because he was a complete asshole, the kind of asshole who caused people to take a dozen or more flights of stairs to their floor to avoid riding in the same elevator and being stuck in his presence during the seemingly endless ascent. The Record Executive lost the respect of his children after the divorce as well. He tried to win them over amid the chaos of the divorce proceedings, attempting to get them to side with him, trying to pit them against their mother by buying them lavish gifts and taking them on extravagant vacations that their mother could not afford. The two older children saw through this facade and quickly sided with their mother, and the two younger children followed suit shortly thereafter, because even though she couldn't buy them the same things the Record Executive could, she could give them the one thing he would never be able to give.

CHANNEL SURFING

Thursday's daylight bid the borough farewell and the evening brought with it an empty apartment. Jody and Michael sat on the stoop in front of Michael's brownstone accompanied by Michael's roommate Evan and their friend Blake. Nighttime noises ate up the air.

Jody was taking long draws from a cigarette, silently reminding himself that he was working through his last pack. It was his third last pack this week.

"Damn you guys look attractive," Jody said, smoke dancing off his lips, up toward his sunglasses, into the evening humidity. "Now remind me: Which one of you is Bell? And which one is Biv? And we already know you're Devoe," Jody said, pointing at Michael.

"This pale mafucka's got jokes," Evan said and threw a half-hearted swing toward Jody. Evan had played guitar for Jody during their touring days. He was slender, a hair under six-feet, dark-skinned, and ivy-league handsome with a jutting-jaw and hard masculine features. Two years ago, Evan and Michael moved to

Brooklyn to further pursue their musical ambitions while Jody and his closest friend Eric stayed in Ohio and pursued a whole lot of nothing. Although the four of them had grown apart over the last few years, it was evident that Michael and Evan had gotten closer; they each had someone to rest their weight on.

"Isn't your birthday coming up soon?" Michael asked Jody.

"Next week."

Twenty-nine?"

"Yeah, rounding out my twenties."

"I'm gon' buy you a tanning-bed membership, Casper."

Jody looked down with a smile and a laugh. Deep cracks in the sidewalk drew patterns of chaos around them.

All three men were a few years younger than Jody: twenty-five, twenty-six. Blake was clearly the most attractive man in the room, regardless of the room: tall and muscular and light-skinned with a close-cropped fade. And he was charming to a fault. Evan met him shortly after they had moved to Brooklyn, a friendship steeped in proximity and convenience, one that didn't seem as if it should last, but it had.

They clustered on the steps, Blake lit a cigarette, Jody lit another.

"Everyone smokes here," Jody said to no one in particular. He ashed his Marlboro and blew smoke at the world.

"And at eleven bucks a pack, why not?" Michael said.

Jody stood up and stretched. The air was crowded with moisture. They were all bored from sitting here, stewing in the evening heat.

"What's on the agenda, Ev?" Blake asked loudly, as though the entire city wanted to know, their collective attention focused on Evan now, waiting for the right answer; there had to be something to do.

"I dunno. Hey, remember them one girls …" Evan trailed off describing a couple college girls. They were both iffy about the names but finally settled on Amy and Asia. Blake commented that the two girls—roommates—didn't live far away, just on the other side of Brooklyn in Flatbush, and he offered to drive the four of them there. Anything to get them off this stoop and out of this heat.

Before they left, they climbed three flights of narrow stairs to Michael's apartment. "I'll be right out. Just need to change my clothes right quick," Michael said, shutting his bedroom door behind him. The three of them sat on the futon, which had doubled as Jody's bed during his stay in Brooklyn, and they waited for Michael. There were cigarette ashes throughout the place. The faux-stainless-steel fridge was tagged with black marker. The recycle bin, trash can, and kitchen sink were all overflowing.

"It smells like regrets in here," Blake said. "It's like someone microwaved a can of body odor, a pack of cigarettes, and a bottle of cheap cologne."

Jody smiled, nodded in agreement. Evan smelled his own armpit and shrugged, satisfied that the smell wasn't emanating from him. Michael exited his bedroom wearing the same exact outfit. He smelled like pot, which no one seemed to notice. The stairs creaked upon their descent from the apartment as they walked to the car, breathing the stale New York air.

Blake cranked the A/C in his late model Toyota 4Runner on their way to Amy and Asia's apartment. A song from a twenty-three-year-old rapper named Drake blasted over the cold air rushing through the vents. Bass rattled the SUV's windows as Blake sang along with the lyrics.

"Shit!" Blake shouted and paused mid-verse. He turned down the stereo while peering in the rearview with wide eyes.

"What you do that for?" Evan asked from the passenger seat, still bobbing his head to a rhythm that was no longer there.

"Look," Blake said, still looking in the rearview, red and blue lights flashing behind them. He'd been going at least twice the speed limit.

"Shit," Michael, Evan, and Jody repeated slowly in a strange multi-tonal unison. Blake rolled down his window and tossed out a half-smoked cigarette. Michael, in the back seat directly behind Blake, also rolled down his window for some reason.

Evan looked over at Blake from the passenger seat and said, "Hey man, I think they got a warrant out on me."

"You got a warrant?" Blake slapped the steering wheel with his open palm.

"Nawl nigga, I'm just playin' wit' cha," Evan said, followed by surround-sound laughter bouncing around the interior of the vehicle.

Blake pulled the car over to the right side of the busy street, half-relieved that Evan wasn't going to jail tonight. It was getting darker outside as dusk blanketed the borough and vehicles sped past violently; their taillights burned red and extinguished themselves as they disappeared into the distance.

The police officer walked up to the window, "I've been waiting on you boys all day." Jody couldn't tell whether he was being a prick or he was just joking.

"We got here as fast as we could, officer," Michael butted in before Blake could say a word.

The officer's name was Kirkendoll according to the nameplate on his chest, an overweight man with a pushed-back hairline that extended his shiny Cro-Magnon forehead to the top of his head. Officer Kirkendoll took one slow step backward and stared at Michael over the aviator sunglasses he was still wearing even though the sun had already died out. Through the vehicle's sunroof, a full-belly moon shone on Brooklyn. A fresh-lit cigarette dangled from Michael's shit-eating grin. He was pleased with his own joke. Blake turned around and mouthed the words "shut up."

"Son, is this a rental car?" Officer Kirkendoll asked Michael. It looked like he was holding back a grin, but if he was, the four of them wouldn't get to see it tonight.

"What?" Michael asked, confused by the question.

"The plates say this is a rental car. Did you know it's illegal to smoke in a rental car in New York?"

"No."

"It is."

Michael was at a loss for words.

"I'm going to need to see your license, son."

Michael grabbed his license, still Ohio issued after a couple years of New York living. The officer stepped up to the driver's window and asked Blake for his license and registration, followed by, "You rented this vehicle?"

"Sort of. I work for a rental car company and they let us use any car we want when we're off duty."

Officer Kirkendoll stepped back for a moment; his boots scraped the concrete. He said something into his shoulder radio, carefully looked over the paperwork and Blake's license and then handed them back. "Do you know how fast you were going, son?"

"No idea, sir."

"You have no idea?" Officer Kirkendoll seemed appalled by this answer.

"No sir."

"Really?"

"Yes sir."

"You don't know how fast you were going?"

"No sir."

"Do you know what the speed limit is on this street?"

"What's that, sir?"

"Do you know what the speed limit is, son?"

"Umm. No sir, I guess I don't."

"It's thirty-five miles an hour."

"Oh."

"I clocked you at seventy-two."

"Seventy-two?"

"Yes. I clocked you driving seventy-two miles an hour in a thirty-five-miles-an-hour zone," the officer said slowly, his New York drawl working its way into his words.

"Sir, there's no way I was going seventy-two."

"Which is it, son?"

"What?"

"Which is it?"

"I'm sorry sir, which is what?"

"You just told me you had no idea how fast you were going," the cop said, "but then you said there was no way you were driving seventy-two miles an hour. Which is it?"

"Sir, I—"

"Either you have no idea or you know for a fact you weren't driving seventy-two."

Blake cut his losses and realized there was no winning this argument. He accepted his speeding ticket and was thankful not to get arrested for doubling the speed limit. Before he walked away, Officer Kirkendoll handed Michael a citation for smoking in a rental. The officer double-tapped the roof of the vehicle and told them to "have a nice day," though his tone suggested otherwise.

Back en route to Amy and Asia's apartment, Michael wadded his citation and tossed it out the window so nonchalantly that he appeared unaware he was doing it. Jody and Evan laughed and Blake quickly accelerated back to sixty-plus miles an hour and switched the music to Notorious B.I.G.'s *Ready to Die*, which blared through the rental car's surprisingly competent sound system.

They arrived in Flatbush a few minutes later and parked at a meter in front of Blake's apartment. They didn't need to pay—it was past billing hours. Michael asked Blake to turn down the music; apparently they'd neglected to inform the girls that they'd soon be visiting. Michael dialed Amy and told her they were coming over. She said she wouldn't be home until at least 10 p.m., which meant they had over an hour to kill.

Blake suggested a quick game of something called "cornhole" on the sidewalk in front of his place. It was a game from Ohio that Michael and Evan had made popular with their friends here in Brooklyn. They went inside to find two large cornhole boards. Blake lived with his older brother, a photographer, in a spacious two-bedroom brownstone: crown molding, restored hardwood floors, high ceilings, a dormant fireplace. Most important, they had air conditioning, albeit a small window unit that did not cool the air throughout the entire apartment, but it was A/C nonetheless.

When he entered the apartment, the cold air coated Jody's lungs and his insides sang with relief. He cherished each breath and held it for a little extra time, an extra moment, waiting to exhale. Blake's brother's photography adorned the walls in every room. IKEA furniture filled the open livingroom/diningroom/ kitchen area. A complex stereo system dripped the percussive noises of rhythm and blues into every room. The place felt appropriately cluttered—a livable, tidy mess.

Michael and Jody dragged the two heavy cornhole boards outside and down the stairs to the sidewalk, each board the size of a dwarf's coffin. Evan and Blake grabbed eight beanbags— four red, four blue. The air was filled with the sounds of the city transitioning from day to night. Passersby gave them odd looks when they started tossing softball-sized beanbags at the five-foot-long wooden boards—Michael and Jody on one team, Blake and Evan on the other. Blake ran back into the apartment and perched two speakers in the open window above the street, providing a hip-hop soundtrack to their game as well as to much of the neighborhood around them. Michael pitched one of his four beanbags. A rap song Jody didn't know played overhead. The sound of a gunshot in Bed-Stuy could not be heard in Flatbush.

"What is you doing?" asked a small black kid walking by. He was maybe six or seven.

"We're playing a game," Jody squatted down to respond.

"What game?"

"It's called cornhole."

"What's that?"

"It's a game we play back in Ohio. It's like horseshoes but instead you throw these beanbags in a hole. Do you like horseshoes?"

"What's that?"

"Umm, OK." Jody stepped back and thought for a moment. "Nevermind about the horseshoes. It's sort of like, umm … I know what, do you like basketball?"

"Yeah!"

"OK, good," he handed the kid a beanbag from his stack. "Then it's like basketball except instead of using a big ball we use these little bean bags and instead of throwing them at a big tall basketball hoop we use these wooden boards with this hole in the middle."

The kid eagerly held the bean bag. It enveloped his hand.

"You want to try?"

His eyes lit up and he nodded his head vigorously.

"Here, let's move you up a little. Now you just throw the bag and try to make it in the hole, and if you get it in the hole you get three points, and if you miss the hole but it lands anywhere on the wood board then you get one point, but if you miss the board *and* the hole then you don't get any points."

"OK!"

"Here, you throw it like this." Jody tossed one bag with an underhanded pitch. It missed the hole but landed on the board. "See, I get one point. Now you try."

The kid tossed his bag with excitement but missed the entire board by several yards. Jody let him try again. On his fifth attempt the little boy made one in the hole and he giggled with victorious excitement, and for a moment, Jody was inside a place that felt right to him, inside this kid's world, a world that accepted him and didn't judge him and somehow understood him. Maybe he'd call his pregnant girlfriend tomorrow to see how she was doing back in Ohio.

During their exchange, half a dozen neighborhood kids and a handful of random adults gathered around to see the alien game. They let a few other kids take their throws and then started their own game illuminated by streetlights under a cloudless sky, the sun long gone but the humidity and heat seemed reluctant to retire. Blake and Evan lost four games in a row, due mostly to Michael's surprising bean-bag-tossing talent. The two losers carried the boards back inside begrudgingly, both claiming bad luck and various interruptions from neighborhood kids as their excuses for their poor showing. Inside, the four of them formed a line to use Blake's bathroom. Jody pissed third and splashed some cold water on his face from the sink. A clock on the wall just outside the bathroom said it was seventeen minutes past ten o'clock.

They piled into Blake's SUV and drove a few blocks to Amy and Asia's place, a distance they could have easily walked. When they arrived, Asia came outside and asked Blake for a ride to a wine shop two blocks away. Asia appeared Iranian or Jewish with doughy facial features that made her look happy. She was well-upholstered, her jeans too snug and the cheeks on her face jiggled when she ran to the car. She was loud and cute, but she looked uncomfortable in her own body. Blake gave her a hard time for not wanting to walk, but he still ran the errand for her, five people sardined side-by-side for two blocks.

The fashionable wine shop's facade was lavender with a large semitransparent artistic rendering of Abraham Lincoln's head etched into the storefront's large main window. From the outside it looked more like a Martini bar or a coffee shop than a wine store. There was no business name anywhere on the building. Asia walked into the store while the four guys sat in the car's air-conditioned interior, lapping up the cool air and staring at her ass in unison as she disappeared into the store. In a few minutes, Asia exited the shop with four bottles of wine, a six-pack of foreign beer, and a bottle of Jim Beam. She got back in the car and offered all four guys a beer, all of whom accepted her offer, except Jody.

"You don't drink?" She asked him, equal parts confused and amused. She was sandwiched between him and Michael in the back seat. She had big dark eyes, highlighted by makeup she didn't need.

"Nope."

"None at all?"

"None."

"What are you a Mormon or something?"

"Something like that."

"He's not a Mormon, Asia," Michael butted in and grabbed a beer from her.

"It's cool, I was just wondering."

"That stuff just messed up a few things in my life. That's all."

"Oh. Sorry about that," she said and opened a beer for herself.

The street noise back at Asia and Amy's apartment echoed differently from Bed-Stuy street noise. It was a two-bedroom brownstone littered with upper-middle-class-college-girl-in-Brooklyn charm. Pottery Barn furniture. Book-lined shelves in the livingroom. Periwinkle window-dressings draped over every window. Empty wine bottles conspired with one another on a solid oak table in the kitchen next to a stack of CDs, Wu-Tang Clan and Dave Matthews Band among them. Amy greeted the quintet at the door, and Jody noticed she wasn't wearing shoes and so he took off his boots before he entered the apartment, even though no one else did, and even though Amy was barefoot she told him to watch for splinters from the floor. She looked at Jody curiously, an extra moment's gaze, like she knew him from somewhere. He didn't remove his sunglasses to return her stare. The six of them congregated in the livingroom and strategically planned the remainder of the evening. It was just after eleven and they all seemed to want to go out and find something better to do.

"Can we smoke in here?" Michael asked.

"If we do it by the window," Amy said.

Michael pulled out his pack of Newports from the cargo pocket of his shorts, grabbed one for himself, and lent one to Evan. They both got their cigarettes going, followed by Amy and Asia, who smoked a brand with a cartoon Indian on the pack. Jody waved off an offer from Amy, "I'm trying to quit. Thanks." Despite the open window, nicotine and carcinogens filled the air, and the smoke couldn't hide his craving. Jody excused himself to use the restroom. Maybe he really could quit this time, or maybe he would've taken one had she offered a Marlboro.

The restroom smelled like a pet shop: the stale odors of cat litter and cat piss wafted in the air around him. Jody used the toilet and rinsed his hands with cold water and then smoothed his hair twice over in the mirror. That couldn't be a gray hair, could it?

By the time he exited the tiny restroom his companions had migrated to Amy's bedroom on the other side of the apartment. Michael and Evan sat Indian-style on the wood floor near the bed. Michael picked at invisible splinters on the ground and ogled Amy sitting cross-legged on her bed. She didn't return his stares. Asia leaned against the windowsill, standing in a pseudo-sitting/standing/leaning position. Nobody mentioned where Blake was; he'd disappeared. Jody walked through the bedroom and sat on the unmade bed next to Amy. She didn't seem to object to inhabiting the same bed as him.

Amy was too thin and bra-less, and she certainly looked the part of a college student—a natural blonde, innocent, twenty-one at best. Two shelves overstocked with books sat above the paper-strewn desk next to the bed: names like DeLillo, Wallace, Franzen, Pynchon, Ellis occupied their creased spines. The screensaver on her computer said *A woman without a man is like a fish without a bicycle* in text that scrolled across the screen. Her pale-blue tank top showed an inch or two of her stomach whenever she reached for something. Short black shorts completed her outfit. She was aloof but in a good way: she seemed to look past everyone, even when she talked to them.

"You read a lot of books," Michael said. He appeared to have a schoolboyish crush on Amy, although they had very little in common in the cultural-tastes department. But he played guitar and sang well, and Jody had learned over the last decade that those two things eliminated nearly all social imperatives when it came to flirting with women, especially girls younger than twenty-five.

"Oh, you read *The Rum Diary*?" Jody asked, picking up a paperback near her pillow, inadvertently interrupting Michael.

"Not yet. I just got it. Did you read it?" she asked.

"I loved it," Jody lied. "Thompson is an amazing writer."

"That's what I hear, but I haven't read any of his stuff," she said.

"And Denis Johnson? You read his stuff?" Jody asked, trying to change the subject from Thompson whom he knew nothing about. He pointed at the three books on her bookshelf, none of which he'd actually read himself, but his ex-wife had told him that Johnson was the "greatest fiction writer alive."

"I love Denis Johnson," she said with excitement.

"He might be the greatest fiction writer alive," Jody said.

"I think so too. What's your favorite book of his?"

"That's a tough call," Jody responded. He looked up at the

ceiling as if mulling over the decision. "Most of his stuff is, I don't know, real intense—it's violent and beautiful. He intertwines the two so well," another comment he'd heard from his ex-wife.

"You're so right about that," she looked at him and only him with her navy-blue eyes.

A brief silence ensued.

"Well, come on, you have to have a favorite," she pressed.

"I don't know. What's yours?"

"You first."

"I really enjoyed *Tree of Smoke*," which was the only title he knew off the top of his head, and he remembered it was a thick book when he saw it on his ex-wife's bookshelf, but he had never attempted to read it, afraid to make such a commitment.

"I liked that one, but it wasn't as good as *Jesus' Son*," she said, not catching on to his lie.

"Like I said—tough call."

She looked him over and Jody looked away.

"So, what's this book about?" he asked, grabbing a nearby book, attempting to remove the pressure to say something witty himself.

"Don't know. Haven't started it yet."

"What does it say on the back?"

"I don't know. I never read the back of books."

"Why? How do you know if you're going to be interested in the book if you won't read the summary?"

"I don't. That's part of the excitement."

"I guess that makes sense," Jody said. "I guess that's the same reason I refuse to watch movie trailers. I don't want to know what the thing's about. I want to find out."

"You don't watch movie trailers?"

"It's like seeing naked pictures of someone—or worse, a sex

tape—before having sex with that person. I simply don't want to know. I want to figure it out on my own."

While the rest of the room happened around them, their conversation progressed. They both talked about other authors whose names festooned the covers of books festooning her shelves; a few of those books Jody had actually heard of and fewer still he'd actually read. She told him about an independent bookstore a couple of blocks down the street and about how she used to date the bookstore's owner's son who now ran the store. She said he gave her most of the books that were now on her shelves, and she joked about the poor bookstore guy, about how he didn't read much even though he ran a bookstore, and how he'd hit on girls by recommending books he hadn't read, or how he pretended to know about particular authors based on what he heard other people say, using the same canned recommendations and cheesy generic synopses of books for different college girls. What kind of lowlife would do such a thing?

Michael and Evan were talking about what they should do tonight, a conversation they'd been having since before they arrived, debating dropping by a club or a bar somewhere nearby, of which there was no shortage of either. They did this often, Jody noticed. They'd be somewhere, and they'd already be planning their next move. It was like real-life channel surfing, always looking for something else, something better, something more than what was already in front of them—whatever they had right there in that moment was never good enough. How often had he done the same thing?

Amy was nursing one of the beers Asia had brought back. "Has anyone ever told you you look like ———?" she asked Jody, mentioning a famous actor's name. She touched the leg of his jeans with her extended bare foot. Jody finally removed his Ray-Bans.

Michael and Evan heard her say this. They looked at each other and laughed loudly.

"No. Never," Jody lied and laughed it off. He'd heard it many times though.

"No, really. You do."

"But he's way shorter than me."

Asia had drunk half her wine bottle in less than an hour. Her eyes were glazed, polished black pearls. She attempted to stand up, not paying much attention to the room around her, fighting gravity's enigma in her tight jeans, which showcased an inch of her buttcrack when she stood. "Where did Blake go?" she asked as she stumbled out of the room, using the shifting walls to guide her way. Michael and Evan followed her out of the room. Evan winked at Jody as he exited.

"Well anyway, you *do*," Amy said.

"Do what?" Jody asked.

"Look like him," she said. "But with nicer hair. Can I touch it?"

"You can touch whatever you want," he said. It was just the two of them now.

"So what do you do?" she asked while touching his mane of hair timidly like she was petting a stray dog, reluctant to appear too forward by running her fingers through his golden strands.

"That's a rather expansive question."

"I mean what do you do for a living?"

"I used to write songs."

"Used to?" she asked, looking at him curiously, her head cocked slightly to the left. "What kind of songs? Oh god, you don't rap, do you?"

"No, I'm afraid I don't," Jody said. "I hope that doesn't disappoint you. I'm more of a simple-sad-love-song kind of guy. You know—guy, guitar, microphone."

"Oh? Really? Like Coldplay or something?"

"Something like that. Darker maybe."

"Darker? What do you mean? You don't strike me as the dark, scary type."

"We just met."

"Well, you don't scare me."

"Maybe you should be scared of me," he smiled.

"I'm going to grab another beer," she said. "You want me to get you anything to drink, anything to eat?"

"No thanks. I'm trying to watch my girlish figure. Maybe a glass of water if it's not too much trouble."

She came back to the room a few minutes later with a beer and a square bottle of water and two CD cases. A look on her face told Jody that she knew something he didn't know—she seemed more excited than before, more alive. She put the two CDs into her stereo and hit a few buttons and soft music permeated the air, something Icelandic, calming background music.

Damn she was young. The more Jody aged, the younger he wanted to be. Amy smelled like smoke and scented lotion, which made him want a cigarette, and her. She sat next to him on the bed, facing him, her knee just barely touching his leg. She examined his tattoos, mouthing a phrase she noticed bonded to him in ink: "It's hard to change when life gets in the way," she read aloud from his arm.

"True indeed," he said and set his water on the floor beside the bed.

"What does that mean?"

"Nothing. Just a lyric from a song."

"What song?"

"My song."

"You sing too?"

"I do. I used to at least."

"Is that why you came to New York?"

"Kind of. I came here to help Michael with some songs. Or I don't know, maybe I came here to get away from whatever I needed to get away from."

"How do you know Michael and those guys? Seems like an interesting relationship."

"We used to play in a band together. Me, Michael, Evan, and my best friend Eric back in Ohio. We were all in a band together."

"Like a high-school garage-band kind of thing?" she said, pulling his leg. "What was the band's name?"

"Umm, actually, *they* were *my* band," he said, embarrassed. He didn't want to sound like he was bragging about having a has-been music career. Plus he was tired of living in the past, and he wanted to change that, but life kept getting in the way. "So I guess *my* name was sort of the band name too. I don't know, it's complicated. It was several years ago."

"*Your* band, huh? So you're like a famous musician then?" she said, ribbing him a little.

"A few years ago I would have said yes to that question, something I'm not proud of now, but I would have said yes. Even though, I wasn't, not really."

She giggled.

"What?" he asked.

"I knew I knew you. They told me out there."

"What?" he asked. "Who?"

"Evan and Michael. When I went out there to get another

beer I asked Michael whether I'd ever met you. I had the feeling I knew you from somewhere. He said of course I knew you, everybody knew you; you're a quote *famous rockstar*, he said, which I laughed at at first but then it clicked—I *did* know you from … from somewhere."

"And where would that be?"

"You just stay the same / never making any sense / You come running back to me / over and over again," she sang his one hit song, off key, delighted that she'd solved the mystery. She didn't have a pretty singing voice, but it didn't matter.

He held back a smile while Amy bent backward reaching for one of the CD cases she'd set down when she reentered the room. She extended her lanky arm as long as she could, exposing her pale stomach and a protruding bellybutton. When she finally got hold of the cracked CD case, she held it up proudly. Jody stared back at himself.

"I see," he said, knowing nothing else to say. He didn't mind cashing in on his notoriety, especially since he hadn't done so when he'd had the chance—back when he was married and faithful and half the girls in the front row wanted to fellate him backstage after each show. But this was different. This was her desire for the old him, a past she couldn't ever be part of. This was him cashing a dead man's check, the burden of former royalty, the cold weight of the crown.

"I thought Michael said your name was Joey when he called —that it was him and Blake and Evan and some guy named Joey that were coming over. I didn't make the connection when you got here, but then I thought I knew you from somewhere, but I didn't know where. Michael—he never told me anything about you or your guys' band or whatever."

"So you used to listen to some of our music?"

"Are you kidding? You're the bad boy from Ohio that I had a crush on in high school," she pointed at the Jody on the album cover.

"High school?" he asked. "You sure you weren't in grade school when that thing came out? How old are you anyway?"

"Old enough," Amy said, but her eyes were uncertain whether this was true. "I really liked that song though. Felt like you wrote it about me and my high-school boyfriend—well one of my high-school boyfriends, anyway."

"I did. Sort of."

"You know what I mean. I could relate to it. That's all."

Jody picked up a paperback book that was folded open beside them on the bed. "What's your book about?" he asked, searching for something clever to say, something that would move their conversation in a different direction.

"Sex," she said with shy grin. "Isn't that what all good books are about? Isn't that what your songs are ultimately about?"

"I don't know. But I think Freud would've agreed with you."

"Asia and the boys are going to a bar down the street," she said, disinterested. "They asked if we were going to join them. But I think we should stay here."

Jody thought about this. He stared over Amy's head for a moment, looking for the right answer on a blank spot on the wall.

"Can you stay?" she asked. "I promise not to bite—unless you're into that sort of thing," she said with the hunger of a man.

Jody looked down and smiled at nothing. He considered playing hard to get for a moment, considered campaigning against the inevitable. But lust conquered every part of him and he didn't put up a fight. While the rest of their party exited the apartment and searched for something better on other channels, Jody decided to be content with the current show playing in front of him, even if it was a rerun. He answered her question by kissing her thin top lip and then her bottom lip, and then their mouths opened and their eyes closed and their tongues met in the middle. Jody pressed his smile against hers, and Amy and her bad boy from Ohio tangled in wrinkled sheets and faked love for an hour. She fell asleep to his racing heartbeat, her head resting on the colorful half heart inked to the wrong side of his chest.

THE ANOINTED ONE

"All these old guys always try to flirt with me. It's so creepy."

"Who, that guy?"

"Yes. And plenty others just like him. They think they can leave me a two-dollar tip and I'll be impressed or something."

"He seemed nice enough to me."

"Just too old, that's all."

"Hey, tread lightly."

"Oh that's right, you're approaching thirty, aren't you?"

"Twenty-nine."

"So almost thirty."

"I might not be as young as all you college girls working at this place, but I'm yet to reach my prime."

"Oh yeah?"

"Yep."

"And you think we're all college girls?"

"Yeah. You're like what, twenty-two, twenty-three?"

"Twenty-four. I'll be twenty-five in a few months."

"See. And your little *barista* co-workers are all about

your age, right? A coffee shop filled with young, attractive Gen Y'ers."

"You know, Courtney is only eighteen."

"Which one is she?"

"Cute, brownish hair, kind of tall."

"Sounds like you're describing yourself."

"Umm, no. She's real thin. Usually wears a ponytail. Kind of quiet."

"Oh yeah, her. She *is* cute. She's only eighteen?"

"Yes."

"Wow, she was born in the nineties then. Maybe I *am* getting old. But then you're proving my point. She's eighteen and she's right around her peak."

"What? So, I'm past my peak then?"

"I didn't say that."

"You know it's not fair, men hit their peak somewhere between twenty-five and forty-five. And women peak somewhere between like twenty-one and—"

"Nineteen?"

"Pervert."

"I'm just giving you a hard time. Anyway, you know I could still totally pass for a college student."

"*Maybe* a grad student, Jody. Maybe."

"Ouch."

"You're too cute."

"Let me ask you something, Leslie."

"What?"

"With that tongue ring, are you able brush your tongue?"

"What?"

"Can you brush your tongue even though you have that tongue ring?"

"Of course I brush my tongue."

"Really? How?"

"What do you mean *how*?"

"Like how do you brush your tongue? Show me."

"Like this …"

"HAHAAHAAAA!."

"Jerk."

"HEEHEEH."

"You're irritatingly charming, Jody. You know that? Anyway, are you going to order something or are you just going to keep laughing? If you haven't noticed, there's a line forming."

"You look good at that, like you've had some practice. And that's not a line behind me—there are two people back there. And both of them are laughing, and I see a smile peaking through on that pretty little face of yours too."

"Whatever."

"I'll take a large coffee. Black."

"OK. Hey I noticed Eric over there. You guys on a man-date?"

"Yeah he likes a little wining and dining before he puts out."

"Quite the salt-and-pepper couple, you two."

"Ebony and Ivory, a beautiful bromance. He's the bottom though. You know that right?"

"For some reason I can't imagine either of you being *the bottom*."

"Thank you?"

"That's two-twenty-five for the coffee."

"Here. You can keep the change."

* * *

"What up, bruh?"

"What's up, Eric?"

"Nothing, nothing. Same shit, different toilet."

"MMMHMMM."

"How 'bout you—you still seeing that one chick?"

"Yeah. That's sort of what I wanted to talk to you about."

"Jolene, right?"

"Yeah. I'm still seeing her. Off and on, but mostly on, you know."

"She was gorgeous, man. You ever get tired of her, make sure you give her my number."

"Come on man."

"Anyway your text said you had some big *revelation.*"

"I do."

"Well?"

"Well, speaking of Jolly, I—"

"Jolly? You call her Jolly?"

"Long story. Don't ask. Anyway, speaking of her, I think I finally figured out women."

"Uh huh."

"Yeah."

"You figured *her* out, or you've figured out *all* women?"

"All women. Well, *women* as in the women in my life anyway."

"You figured them out? What does that even mean?"

"Figured them out is probably the wrong way to say it. How about: I figured out my problem with women."

"That sounds more honest."

"OK, I realize this might sound a bit narcissistic but—"

"Oh boy."

"What?"

"Nothing. Go ahead."

"Anyway, this might sound narcissistic but women always fall in love with me. Every time. Without fail."

"MMMHMM. That's your *revelation*? Here I'll show you your text message. You said *revelation*. And this is it?"

"Seriously. It's like they can't help but to fall in love with me."

"A *bit* narcissistic? This? Noooooooo. I personally knew it was just a matter of time before you realized that you're God's gift to women."

"So it sounds conceited or dick-headed I know, but I didn't mean for it to be this way. It just is."

"So that's it: Jody Grafton, the anointed one. Oh the burden that must be."

"Yeah, well. Odd thing is—at least to me—is that I'm a totally average guy."

"Average? You think you're an *average* guy?"

"Yeah. Totally average."

"Like average as in *normal*?"

"No. Like average as in average. Like I'm nice to women—I don't yell at them, I try to listen, all that bullshit—but that's nothing special. And I'm an average looking guy. You know, just average."

"Uh huh. *Average*."

"What? Why you looking at me like that?"

"Are you kidding me, Jody?"

"What? No. Anyway it usually has something to do with the way I look at them. Least that's what they tell me. Like that I stare at them, make them feel like they are the only person on earth. The only thing that matters. And hell they might be the only thing that matters at the time. But the problem is that it's completely unintentional and it never lasts."

"What's unintentional? You look at them unintentionally?"

"No. The way I make them feel. I've been told this by a few girls but never connected the dots until the other day when I sent you that text."

"This is really what they tell you? You've been told this by more than one woman?"

"Yes. Several. In their own little ways."

"Maybe you just sell them a bill of goods, Jody. You ever think of that?"

"I don't know. I don't think so. I guess I do want to be loved though. Even if I don't love them. Or maybe I do love them. Truth be told, I think I've loved every woman I've ever met, even when they don't love me back."

VARIOUS COLORS OF PAINT ON THE SPILL CANVAS

Jody woke with Amy on his breath and a cigarette on his mind. The air conditioner in her window hummed a somber baritone. Amy lay there beside him, her head pressed against his arm, hair everywhere. Hints of sunlight leaked through the curtains and into the room, painting the break of day. Her calm, lonely breaths seemed to be raising the sun from its slumber. It was no longer night, but the day wasn't yet here either—it was that delicate time in-between, blending the darkness with the light.

Jody moved his arm from under Amy's sleeping head, slipped out of bed, and put on his blue jeans and his wrinkled teeshirt and tiptoed out of the bedroom to use the restroom. In the mirror, his hair was matted to his head; he attempted to fix it using his fingers as a makeshift comb, and then he walked through the hallway and into the livingroom but didn't see anyone lingering from the night before. Uncertain of where everyone had gone, he laced his Redwings and didn't bother to say goodbye. The door creaked when it shut behind him.

Michael's first solo acoustic show was that night, opening for The Spill Canvas, an alt-rock band with too many guitars. Soundcheck wasn't till 7 p.m., so to kill time Jody and Michael, along with Blake and Evan, stopped by Enclave, a nightclub a few blocks from Blake's apartment. The place was already overflowing with patrons at 5 o'clock, and there was a fifteen-minute wait to get in the door, but they were able to circumvent the line because the owners of the nightclub knew Blake, whose brother had done the photography for Enclave's website, and Blake's picture was featured on their flyers, posters, and other promotional materials.

After checking Jody's ID at the venue's entrance, the large black doorman eyeballed Jody's tattoos and seemed particularly interested in the bird-winged airplane flying on his left arm. He handed Jody's driver's license back and asked him whether he wanted to purchase some cocaine. "No thanks. I'm waiting for these pills to kick in," he said, politely declining the doorman's offer, though this was a lie: the pills had *already* kicked in, which gave everything a kinesthetic edge. Jody wanted to touch everything at once. He resisted grabbing the doorman's large bicep as he took back and pocketed his ID.

Less than an hour earlier, without asking what they were, Jody had taken two large pills from Blake, though he wasn't sure why. Maybe it was because he was feeling good and he wanted to prolong that feeling, or maybe he wanted to change his state, or maybe he had terrible will power. Whatever his reasoning, he was now feeling the effects of those pills. So were Evan and Blake, even though they didn't show it—but then again, they took only one pill each, and Michael had declined the offer since he had to be on stage in a few hours.

They entered an open room with low light, fresh paint, and

newer fixtures. The place smelled like a sad song: spilled drinks, bad breath, cigarette smoke working its way in from outside. Despite the line out the door, which was apparently just for show, there were only thirty-or-so people inside, all of whom looked like they didn't belong here: burly men in their forties and fifties wearing leather jackets and drinking Budweisers; a handful of semi-attractive party-weathered women in their late twenties and early thirties wearing bikini tops and jean shorts and flip-flops; one guy wearing a spiked collar working behind the bar; and about a dozen co-ed college students who had apparently all received different versions of the bar's dress code, from button-down shirts and fashionable summer dresses, to tattered teeshirts with mesh basketball shorts and Birkenstocks.

With Blake leading their way they formed an ad hoc four-man single-file line and walked toward the back door. Remixed versions of popular eighties songs filled the warm dense air, peppered with loud conversations of people attempting to talk over the blaring music. Currently, a techno version of Corey Hart's "Sunglasses At Night" sucked the sound out of the room. Jody heard the lyrics but didn't remove his Ray-Bans. Mr. Hart sung over everyone's chatter: *Don't masquerade with the guy in shades, oh no.* As they walked, it seemed like one out of every two people in this place stopped Blake to say hello or to ask him a question. Jody saw their lips moving, but he couldn't hear what they were saying over the rattle of the beat. *Don't be afraid of the guy in shades, oh no.* It took more than five minutes to make it to the back of the room; Blake's provisional entourage stood awkwardly behind him as he stopped and talked over the music. *'Cuz you got it made with the guy in shades, oh no.* They walked past the bar to the back door; it opened to a large fenced-in patio area half-covered in thick sand, the remnants of an outdoor sand volleyball court, no volleyball net or volleyball ball in sight. The volume of the music lessened out here, but it still controlled the ambience. Jody pushed his Ray-Bans up on the bridge of his nose. *And I wear my sunglasses at night, so I can, so I can, see the light that's right before my eyes.* Their single-file line dispersed when they reached the patio, and Michael and Jody ended up next to a wooden fence near the back, talking about nothing for a while.

"Fairly eclectic group here tonight," Jody said.

"Bunch of weirdos if you ask me." Michael looked around.

"I have to piss," Jody mentioned after a minute of silently sneering at Enclave's patrons.

"What?" Michael asked.

Jody, submerged in cacophonous eighties techno and the pull of the pills, ventured back into the club and into the pale light of the men's room. There was a condom dispenser on the wall near the sink and next to it a guy stood directly in front of a single-spray cologne dispenser spreading apart the collar of his shirt and exposing his chest to make certain he got every penny's worth of his seventy-five cents of scented mist. A post-election poster of Barack Obama on the wall above the urinal had the word DOPE! typeset beneath an artistic rendering of the President's bust. Scribbled on the bathroom wall in thick black graffiti were the words PLEASE STOP WRITING ON THE WALLZ.

"Are you going to piss for both of us?" a deep voice said from somewhere in the restroom. Jody finished his business at the urinal, turned around and saw a burly man in his forties with a week's worth of facial hair; he was holding his crotch and bouncing up and down like a boy who was still figuring out his bladder. Jody zipped his fly and resisted the urge to pet this man's face. He rinsed his hands in the sink and could smell a deluge of stale cologne still lingering from the machine on the wall.

A manic woman stopped Jody on his return trip to the patio. She looked thirty-something and ruggedly pretty, though he wasn't sure whether his standards had been lowered under the fog of the pills. She grabbed his arm and stopped him as he walked by and asked him a question he couldn't understand over an electronic version of Cindy Lauper's "Girls Just Want to Have Fun": *Came home in the middle of the night, father says what you gonna do with your life?* She was wearing a pink bikini top and an innie bellybutton and a gap-tooth smile. Her perfume smelled like insecurity. Jody smiled back at this woman as her mouth presented another string of inaudible words. She clutched his left bicep with her right hand, while her other hand held tightly the thick metal railing behind her as if it was preventing her from slipping into the deep end. She looked like she wanted to tell somebody her life story. *Well mother dear we're not the fortunate ones, oh girls they want to have fun.* This woman kept talking, coughing up the damage, her lips moving without producing any sounds, and now she was holding his other bicep, she was somehow holding both of his biceps now, although her left hand still appeared to be hanging on to the railing, and he wasn't sure how she was doing this, but her touch made him want her, and he noticed himself swelling in his pants.

"Are you ready?" God said into Jody's ear. But then it wasn't God at all. "We gotta get outta here." It was Michael's voice in his ear, and he was letting him know it was time to go. Ushered by Michael's clenching hands, Jody slipped out of the pink-bikini woman's grip while her silent life story continued to slip out of her moving lips, lips painted the color of the apocalypse.

"I love you," Jody said to the woman, and he meant these words, as Michael tore him away and they rejoined their group. They saw the same large doorman when they approached the exit, and Jody thought about maybe taking him up on that offer to buy some coke, even though he didn't particularly like cocaine and he hadn't done a line in years. Outside, Jody noticed Amy from last night standing in line, but she didn't notice his notice. From here she looked like the most beautiful girl in the world. Enclave's door was still open and music spilled out onto the street as Blake and Michael and Evan moved in slow motion around Jody. When he saw Amy, he attempted to point at her to show the guys she was here, but his hands didn't cooperate with his head. He wanted to yell an apology for last night, for not reading any of the books he had lied about; he wanted to say he was sorry and confess that he had never read anything by Don DeLillo, and he wanted to tell her he'd never even heard of Dave Thomas or David Wallace or *fuck* … whatever his name was, but instead he yelled, "You're still lonely, right?" at the top of his lungs toward the entire line. And now she noticed him, dragging last night into the present. The past is never where you want to leave it.

As they drove away, Jody rolled down his backseat window and said, "I'll see you around," when they passed Amy, but he actually meant to say "goodbye." The wind through the open window was sobering and terrifying as they drove from Brooklyn to Manhattan. "What was in those horse-pills you gave me," Jody asked Blake, who was behind the wheel.

"Mescaline and ground-up mushrooms," someone who sort of looked like Evan said from the passenger seat. "But you weren't supposed to take both of them. One will do you up good."

Jody stuck his arm out the window and when the car came to a stop at a red light he heard the roadside crickets turn on their charm. He waited for the moon to swallow him through the open sunroof, to have its way with him. He worked his phone out of his pocket and tried to make some sense out of the mystery of its buttons. He wanted to make a phone call, wanted to call someone to help put his heart back together, but even if the buttons on the phone weren't melting, he didn't have anyone to call, so he crammed the device back into his pants before it turned into a spider or a bat or some other horrifying, lonely creature. He looked around the car: the world around him wanted to tell him something, but he didn't want to hear it, so he hid behind his eyelids and found solace.

When Jody regained consciousness, he was standing in a large open space and Michael was on a stage in front of him with a guitar singing one of his songs in front of a microphone. Was this already soundcheck? This place seemed crowded for a soundcheck. He needed something to lean on, so he pushed his way through the crowd toward the bar. There were young women everywhere. The height of his terrifying buzz seemed to have dissipated, but he wasn't sure based on the crowd congregating around him. There were attractive lesbians everywhere, a feat he'd never witnessed in real life. Only in pornographic films did lesbians look this attractive. Near the bar, two sets of two twenty-two-year-old girls kissed each other with open mouths and then switched partners and did the same thing. It was impossible for Jody not to gawk at this spectacle. Next to the lipstick quartet, a heavyset butch woman palmed the ass of her tiny, beautiful girlfriend while Michael's voice filled the air around them. In the corner shadows, over on the other side of the bar, a young homely girl cried to herself beneath the darkness and the sad songs; she looked like she'd been crying her entire life. Jody placed his sunglasses on top of his head and violently rubbed his eyes. He leaned on a structural support beam, looking around panoramically, attempting to make sense of the scene around him.

At first he was massively aroused by this excessive girl-on-girl action, but then reality washed over him: this must be what Hell is like—hoards of attractive women who wanted nothing to do with him, and no matter how hard he'd try, they'd never be interested in his advances. But then this realization was strangely calming since it seemed to remove all the social pressure and pretense from the evening, like he'd woken in a place in which he was no longer on a mission to find a lock to fit his key, and so he could focus on the moment, he could focus on having a good time without the pressure of trying to get laid. This was a feeling he hadn't felt before. Perhaps Hell had its benefits.

And then a strong hand grabbed his shoulder from behind and Jody flinched forward abruptly. Nothing around him made sense, and it made even less sense because he didn't think he was feeling the pills as much anymore. No phones were melting in his hand, he wasn't crying out incoherently, and he seemed to have all his fingers now. His next instinct was to turn around swinging at the man or woman or thing attached to the hand that grabbed him.

"Whoa, cowboy! Still feeling the pills?" It was Evan who'd grabbed his shoulder.

"What?" Jody asked, even though he'd heard every word of the question. He unclenched his fist but was still grimacing from Evan's unexpected touch. "Why are so many people here for the soundcheck?"

"Soundcheck? What are you talking about? This is the real

thing—this is the show. You were asleep on a couch in the back for soundcheck. We got to meet the guys from Spill Canvas."

"Who?"

"The Spill Canvas—the band Michael's opening for. Great group of guys. Michael's set just started. Let's get closer." Evan put his arm around Jody and ushered him toward the stage, working their way through a crowd that seemed to be composed of fifty percent lesbians, mostly beautiful college girls with a few older butch women peppered in the mix; twenty-five percent strange young men wearing eyeliner and all black with definite psychological issues; and twenty-five percent seemingly normal people like Jody and Evan, all of whom looked confused by the other seventy-five percent. After a minute of wading through the crowd, they found a place to stand, a couple cute college girls in front of them held hands and listened to Michael's every word, as did the girls in front of those girls. It reminded Jody of some of his early shows, where he'd opened for national acts, which always felt like a strange proposition back then, forcing an audience to listen to forty minutes of music they never signed up to listen to in the first place. It felt like asking a girl to a dance that you knew she didn't want to attend, but she went anyway because a different guy would be there.

Jody and Evan considerately observed Michael's set, beautiful song by beautiful song. Strangely, so did most of the lesbians and the rest of the crowd; they were into it, they liked Michael and this made Jody feel a strange kind of pleasure. He wasn't used to feeling good for someone else. The concert hall was more than half full, and people were still piling in through the front doors. Michael gave it his all; he had played in front of larger crowds before, but not solo, and certainly not as the center of attention. Things change when you're in the spotlight—the lights shine brighter, the sounds get louder, your saliva tastes more metallic, every damaged fiber of your being feels naked and exposed to the world.

Jody looked to his right and there she was. It was the girl from his bus ride to Brooklyn two days prior, which now seemed like forever ago—the girl in the white summer dress, the girl from his dream who explained his entire life in the breath of a single sentence, the girl who gave him the wrong damn phone number. *Shelly*. She was dancing by herself near the bar, wearing the same white dress as the other day. He fixed his gaze and couldn't stop watching her dance. She moved elegantly. Jody stared but she didn't notice him or anything outside herself. A world of emotions swelled up inside him. He was frustrated she'd given him the wrong number, but he was also confused as to why she would show up here after giving him the wrong number. But he was also excited for a second chance. She must be here for him; he's the one who invited her, after all. Overwhelmed with rejection and trepidation, two emotions he wasn't used to, he approached her reluctantly. Eric stayed near the stage with his arms crossed, looking up, keeping his eyes on Michael as Jody meandered through the crowd toward Shelly. Something about this girl was different, a tune he couldn't name. Her eyes were closed and her torso swayed like a serpent charmed by the sounds of music. Was she really here? The pills had worn off considerably, and yet here she was in front of him, tiny and brilliant, an overhead light accenting her body, adding an seraphic aura to the area in which she moved. He stepped into her personal space, his thoughts heavy with hope, but she didn't open her eyes—she was one with the music. Jody inched so close that he could count every freckle on her face. She possessed a womanness so powerful that it encompassed both sexes: she was strong, and yet she was beautiful. He wanted to tell her how beautiful she was, not just to walk in her good graces but because he sincerely meant it. And with this thought, her eyelids slowly opened, exposing her bright green eyes. She smiled as if she'd known he'd been there in front of her the entire time.

"Would you like to dance?" Shelly asked.

"For the rest of our lives?" Jody wasn't sure why these words left his mouth.

"How about the rest of this song?" She laughed a private-school laugh.

"I don't dance."

"That's a shame," she said. Jody watched her mouth let go of these words as she backed away slowly, as if walking on water, not breaking eye contact.

"Dancing's like walking a tightrope," he said, though he wasn't entirely sure what he meant by this either.

"Then walk the tightrope with me."

"What if we fall?"

"We'll fall together."

Jody followed. "We should run away together," his mouth was leaking words that hadn't yet filtered through his brain.

She hovered back toward him. What made her come closer? He wasn't sure what love was, but maybe it felt like this. Or was it lust that burned off the fog of his thoughts? Or were love and lust the same thing?

"I think He's calling your name," Shelly said.

"What?"

"The man on stage—your friend—it sounds like he's calling your name."

Jody turned and looked up at Michael in front of the

microphone. "I'd like to sing a song with my friend." He motioned at Jody, directing him toward the stage not unlike an air-traffic controller. "Let's get him up here. It's a song you might know. If you know the words, sing with us. Hell, if you don't know the words, you can still sing."

Jody turned back to say something—anything—to Shelly, to tell her not to go anywhere, that he'd be right back. But when he did, he just saw Evan, who grabbed his arm and was now leading him to the stage. Jody looked back over his shoulder, scanning the expanding crowd for Shelly, but he couldn't find her in the sea of strange people.

On stage, Michael said, "This is a song called 'Ohio Again,' by my good friend Jody Grafton." He dropped back and played the first few chords of the song that had spawned Jody's one-hit career; he left Jody in the spotlight, in front of the microphone. Muscle memory took over and Jody was instantly transported back to the limelight, back to the days when he'd performed in front of large crowds who begged for this one song. He looked out at the audience. He could hardly see them, but there must've been 2,000 people here. He wrapped his right hand around the mic without thinking—he no longer had to think—and he closed his eyes and sang the first two lines:

What I need is
You by my side

After the first two verses, Michael joined him, standing in solidarity in front of the mic stand and its single microphone, singing the chorus in unison with the crowd:

You just stay the same

never making any sense
You come running back to me
over and over again

The crowd ate it up. They'd all been through frustrating relationships and every person in here could identify with this sentiment. Or maybe it was them who were staying the same, clinging to the past, afraid of change. Michael played the guitar and Jody held the microphone toward the crowd as they chanted these lines over and over, and then there she was—Shelly, standing in the crowd, her white dress a canvas to a spectrum of color.

A NEW DAY AT MIDNIGHT

It had been silent on the subway. What a nice surprise. Jody Grafton hadn't realized this silence until now, after already exiting the train. He was now approaching Times Square, swimming vigorously against the stream of people and the spill of electric light, beneath the howl of the world, the sounds of a city dead inside. The lights seemed to ripple in the high-noon heat, bending and flickering and dancing all around him, overwhelming and unforgiving, sucking the polluted oxygen from the air, spitting fluorescent fumes, a rainbow of glow that rivaled the sun in the cerebral sky overhead.

The past was the past. The past was nothing at all now. His mother was dead, the cancer had taken her life, and nothing was going to bring her back. His marriage was over, and his ex-wife deserved to be happy, even if that meant she was happy with someone else, someone other than him, someone with a different last name and a house and some children and all the things she wanted, doing all the things he had refused to do to make her happy. Jody could keep his eyes on the road now, ignoring the rearview and the rubble behind him. If he went back to Ohio, he would have to deal with only the present—and simply hope for the best on the wide open road ahead. His unborn child. His miserable girlfriend. His failed musical career. These were all things he could deal with. The worst was behind him. After the last two days of songwriting and performing on stage—his first foray into music in over three years—the energy was back. He felt uxorious for the songs again—electric, like the digital billboards that besieged the cityscape surrounding him now. He breathed in the light while car horns attacked eardrums and muffled a million conversations transpiring on every sidewalk in this place. The enmity of noise made him yearn for the euphony of silence. But this was the opposite, the antithesis of solitude and calm. It was crazy-making. He closed his eyes and imagined himself cupping his hands over his ears and screaming at the top of his lungs. But he refrained.

He opened his eyes. Was that Michael Jackson who just walked by? It couldn't be. Michael Jackson must have been dead for at least a year now.

Jody felt older than he used to, but in a good way: more mature, less impulsive, better adjusted. There was a glimpse of his reflection in a storefront window and he noticed that he looked older too. He was about to turn twenty-nine in a week, and the hardest and most arduous and in many ways most surreal years of his life were behind him.

God, it was hot. Why was he sweating more than he used to? Perhaps even his pores were maturing. Earlier that morning, while picking at his face in the mirror at his friend Michael's apartment, he noticed his boyish appearance and baby's-bottom skin had hardened a bit. Some of his older tattoos were fading.

The musical notes on this right arm would need to be filled in with fresh ink soon.

He'd been here for less than a week, and he'd already had enough of this place. If home is where the heart is, then his heart was not in New York. Venturing back to Ohio felt like the right move now. Times Square was just the tipping point. He felt enveloped by this rapacious city. There was nowhere to turn for solace.

Earlier that morning, on his way to the J train, a homeless man had tried to sell him an *Ally McBeal* VHS tape. Apparently Jody looked like the kind of guy who still owned a VCR, and he must've looked like an *Ally McBeal* fan, as well. But then aren't all white people *Ally McBeal* fans? If so, then he was the only *Ally McBeal* fan in sight in Bed-Stuy Brooklyn that morning as he walked to the train, past a newish McDonalds and an old Walgreens and a United States Post Office with barred windows that was closed at 11 a.m. and a fast food restaurant called Tasty Chicken and a few dozen indistinguishable storefronts selling incense and beads and liquor and candy and fruit. It was late June, New York summer, one-hundred-and-one degrees with humidity, the air was waterlogged and dense. He used to watch *Ally McBeal* with his mother when he was little, that and *60 Minutes*, which he hated as a kid, except Andy Rooney at the end of each episode, which felt like the big payoff for laboring through 58 minutes of tedium, 58 minutes of reductive nonsense for a two-minute payoff. He declined the offer to purchase the VHS and then wondered whether Andy Rooney was still alive. Those eyebrows of his, they were tentacles, he was a mad man. It was all part of his disheveled image: the Lilliputian office, the books scattered about, the organized clutter, the lonely mayhem of Andy Rooney.

An aggressive beggar approached Jody near the stairway entrance to the train station. "Hey white boy, give me a quarter!" He shoved a dirty Styrofoam cup in his direction.

Jody looked at him through dark sunglasses. "How did you know my name?"

"Huh?"

"Do you have any change?" Jody asked him. "I need it for the train."

The homeless man walked away confused and mumbled something that sounded a lot like *Fuck you white boy.*

Today was Saturday. He had been here since Wednesday, but four days seemed like a week in this city. This morning, Jody decided to see Times Square before he went to the recording studio to help Michael record his album. He'd been to New York a handful of times, playing shows at the height of his career, but he'd never made it to Times Square. There's no real reason for anyone to visit Times Square other than the obligatory trip one must take whenever one visits New York City.

Exit the J train. Subway station. Grand Street. Arenose black train tracks below, gum-stained concrete above, subway-tile-lined walls throughout (subway tile in the subway, go figure). Is this Chinatown? An old Asian man played Far-Eastern music on what looked like a giant banjo. It was the only value-adding form of panhandling Jody had witnessed this entire trip. A rat meandered through the tracks below. Two teenage black girls laughed and pointed at the rat below and pretended to be grossed. On the platform, it was just those two girls and Jody towering over a crowded sea of Asian subway passengers. D train to 34th Street. Exit the train. A female cop was taking a picture of another female cop standing next to a young, glittery Michael Jackson, clearly an imitation Michael Jackson. What was going on? It turned out that Michael Jackson had been dead for exactly one year to the day, which meant Jody saw no less than a dozen Michael Jacksons today, all ranging from various periods in his career: there was the young Jackson 5 Michael Jackson with the flat nose and afro, the young but mature *Thriller* Michael Jackson in which the first hints of his lifelong metamorphosis peaked through in his sculpted nose and his changed hair, the *Bad* Michael Jackson with his lighter skin and longer hair and more Anglo features, and the androgynous *Dangerous* Michael Jackson with his long shiny hair and his oddly constructed face and, and … and *that* nose. Unbelievable. That nose, nearly gone. A black man from Gary Indiana somehow became a white woman in California over time. Only in America. The Michael Jackson in front of him now looked like Michael Jackson just after *Thriller* but before *Bad*, meaning a louder, more opulent wardrobe but still little change in his facial structure. Michael Jackson had been larger than life; it was hard for Jody to believe he had died at all. He remembered it well though: his mother was dying when Michael Jackson passed. Every media outlet eulogized him for days after his death, replaying his life on every station. Flipping through the channels, death was unavoidable. Jody could recall the look on his mother's face when she saw this aftermath. That was the moment she realized she was dying, not just in the figurative sense, but she herself was dying, and she knew it. An expression broke across her face, a dichotomy of fear and acceptance. She died a few months later, to far less fanfare than MJ. But that was the past, and the past no longer existed, Jody reminded himself.

From the subway station, he ascended a perpetual flight of stairs, searching for some surface air. A portly older woman with a heavy Eastern European accent walked down the stairs in the opposite direction. She stopped Jody and said, "I am not here," an esoteric declaration, a confusing paradox. Except it sounded more like "I am not here?" and she seemed to be asking Jody where she was or whether she was going in the right direction.

"Yes you are. You *are* here, honey," he said and touched her arm softly and kept walking up the stairs. He was in no position to give directions.

He emerged from the subterranean congestion and heat and humidity to the New York City street-level congestion and heat and humidity. He was out of breath, so he paused and thought about lighting a cigarette. He was quitting, he told himself, and he resisted the burning urge to light up. The white sun overhead made his eyes water, even through his Ray-Bans.

The ratio of beautiful women to not-beautiful women walking the Avenue of the Americas was staggeringly positive. Walking north he saw a catatonic homeless man holding a cardboard sign that said NEED MO PENNIES. A few blocks down, a rambunctious panhandler sat in a wheelchair and smiled and laughed to himself with a sign propped on his lap: GIVE ME MONEY OR I WILL KICK YOU IN THE FACE. The man had no legs.

Jody could feel beads of sweat begin to pool and trickle down the small of his back as he negotiated his way through a crowd of Wayfarer sunglasses and skinny cuffed jean shorts and deep-V-neck teeshirts and white earbuds jammed into ears and Chuck Taylor sneakers and colorful tattoo sleeves and gingham dress shirts tucked into crisp slim khakis and leather messenger bags and more cute summer dresses than he could count. A businessman walked past speedily and rattled off a string of incoherent business cliches in rapid succession into his cellphone: "... yes, we'll need to *ramp up our distribution* ...

sounds like we're *locked and loaded* then … we can *circle back* and *touch base* in the *a.m.* … the *bottom line* is we had to *drop the hammer* on him … this is a *high-level initiative* from the *top down* … we'll be *bringing our A-game* … we just have to *keep our eye on the ball* … *et cetera, et cetera, et cetera* …" He actually said *et cetera* three times in a row, mid-rant, without stopping to take a breath. Jody kept walking north, resisting the urge to punch this man in the face. Up ahead, a Hispanic man accidentally dropped a half-eaten mango while crossing the street and was almost careened by a tan Volvo stationwagon as it ran a yellow light. The Volvo's bumpersticker said *Dear Hipsters, We Used to be just like you. Sincerely, The Yuppies.*

On the next block, a blind man stood against a brick wall, holding a ragged paper cup and a sign that didn't ask for money but said YOU ARE LOVED EVEN IF YOU DON'T REALIZE IT. His cane leaned against the wall beside him and Jody thought the blind man might honestly be able to see better than him, better than most people within this Saturday Babylon, and so out of guilt he placed a twenty-dollar bill inside the man's cup and then immediately regretted it, second guessing his decision because he didn't know whether the man was truly blind or just faking it and twenty dollars was a lot of money and he might need it later and what if the man really was blind but planned to use the money for alcohol or heroin which meant Jody was just adding to the problem, a willing accomplice to a victimless crime.

During his short walk to Times Square Jody was handed no less than half a dozen flyers containing attractive girls possessed by lifeless facial expressions standing in provocative poses. Here he was, standing in the midst of the mayhem, his pupils dancing in the overwhelming luminescence, wondering why he had even bothered to come here. Times Square itself was anticlimactic; it felt like it was set up to be this way, to leave a void you had to fill by buying stuff, stuff that was advertised on every flat surface in sight. It was the absolute epitome of opulence and consumerism and the hard-to-explain pernicious side of capitalism. And it did an outstanding job doing what it was designed to do, to overwhelm people's senses with slick, cool, hip, new, trendy marketing. It was like trying to drink from a fire hose: more than you'd ever need, but it could never slake your thirst for more. It was painful if you were aware of what was going on, emotionally abortive if you weren't. Jody spent less than ten minutes in Times Square, the entire time questioning why he wanted to visit it in the first place, and he then planned his trek back to Brooklyn to meet Michael in a studio in Crown Heights. He took the train to Delancey station, Delancey to Allen Street, still in Manhattan. Pitstop at Starbucks. Jody swore he heard the girl in front of him order a "Venti Husband," while he himself ordered a Tall Black Eye, which basically was just a small coffee with two shots of espresso, but the girl behind the counter must've been new here because she laughed and thought he ordered a Tall Black Guy, a mistake she looked embarrassed about. Taking the joke a step further, Jody asked her whether she could wheel out Manute Bol's corpse from the stock room, but the young girl didn't know who Manute Bol was. Nevermind, he told her and paid for his coffee and then asked for the key to the restroom.

At the studio later that afternoon, Jody helped Michael refine a few songs for Michael's debut album. Michael sat on a stool in the recording booth, looking like a young Larry Fishburne, holding an acoustic guitar on this lap. Jody sat with

Michael's manager, Wes, and the recording engineer in the main sound room. He stayed out of the way as he listened to Wes argue with the engineer about the mix. He had all the makings of a good manager. Jody wished his old manager would've been half the advocate Wes was. It seemed to Jody that Wes was one of those rare finds, a manager who loved the music, had a passion for helping artists grow, and had enough business sense and connections within the industry to make stuff happen.

A rough cut of Michael's song played over the studio's speakers. A recorded Michael sang a line that Jody wrote for him: "I can see these streetlights pass me by / driving from the darkness, make my way toward the light." His voice sounded like early David Gray with more soul. Jody was impressed by how much Michael had matured and improved over the last few years since they'd worked together. Back then, it was Michael sitting the bench, listening to Jody record his first, second, and third albums, helping with background vocals and some instrumentation when needed. But now Michael was in the foreground, this was *his* time, and Jody wanted to be there to support him however he could.

"That piano is too loud," Wes told the engineer, pointing at the studio monitors. "Bring it down. It's supposed to be more subtle, in the background."

"If I turn it down much more you're not going to be able to hear it at all," the engineer said.

"I didn't ask you to turn it down *much* more. I just asked you to turn it down."

The engineer fiddled with two of the giant soundboard's crossfaders.

"See, that's better," Wes said, looking back at Jody rhetorically. "That's what I'm talking about. Subtle, a little eerie."

Jody nodded. Wes was good. The piano moaned a pillowy ache beneath the more prominent acoustic guitar while Michael's vocals occupied center stage. His voice was the obvious star of the show.

Michael's roommate, Evan, walked into the studio with an electric guitar. He was here to overlay chords on four songs. Wes had, using his own money, hired someone to play violin and cello on three of the tracks, as well. Despite his initial reservations, Jody genuinely liked Wes now.

Michael walked out of the recording booth, into the sound room, and presented Evan with a standard masculine half-hug handshake. Jody and the engineer were the only white guys in the room, though Jody identified much more with his darker-skinned counterparts than the overweight middle-aged man in front of the soundboard. Michael sat next to Jody on the couch in the back.

"That was amazing," Wes told Michael and took a sip of bottled water. "You nailed it on that song."

"Thanks," Michael said. "Hey Jody, I need help with some of these lines." He handed Jody a weathered spiralbound notebook with a torn red cover. It was bursting with words, lyrics filled every page.

"Anything for you, you handsome bastard." Jody looked down at the paper and most of the words were crossed out or sloppily rewritten or just completely incomprehensible. "Did you have a kindergartner transcribe your lyrics for you, Mikey?"

"What are you talking about? That's some penmanship right there. Dayton Public Schools at its finest," Michael said, tapping his finger on the page. "You know I graduated from seventh grade—twice."

"That's 'cause you failed the first time," Evan piped in from a few feet away.

"Details, details. Anyway, can you help me with these lyrics or what?"

"Yeah, I can help," Jody said and then loudly asked the room, "Who has a giant eraser?"

Michael shoved Jody playfully. They spent the next two-and-a-half hours rewriting lyrics to four songs. Wes informed them that they had two more days of studio time after today to finish the initial recordings. Five songs were already in the bag, and they had six more to go. Michael assured Wes it wouldn't be a problem. Wes looked at Jody to verify the accuracy of Michael's assurance.

"We're golden," Jody said with a pen clenched between his teeth. "My patchwork is nearly done here."

Michael re-inhabited the recording booth and sang the new lyrics, fingerpicking his Gibson, belting out haunting melodies over several takes. Wes had him record and re-record everything, sometimes dozens of times, until it felt right. Whenever Wes thought Michael had nailed a particular part, he asked him to move on to the next song.

By six in the evening their studio time was over. Michael, Wes, and Evan invited Jody to join them to celebrate the seven songs they had in the bag.

"Love to but I can't. I've got plans tonight," Jody said.

"Plans?" Michael asked.

"Yeah. I saw Shelly last night at your show."

"Who?"

"Shelly. The girl I told you about from the bus to Brooklyn. The girl who gave me the wrong number."

"You're going out with a girl that gave you a wrong number? Are you stupid or somethin'?"

"I don't think you—"

"You think she's going to show up?" Michael asked, tapping Jody's shoulder with his index finger to add emphasis to each word that followed: "She. Gave. You. The. Wrong. Number."

"No, you see, she—"

"That means she don't want nothin' to do with you."

"She didn't—"

"Man, that's borderline stalking, going to see a girl that gave you the wrong—"

"Michael—shut up," Jody interrupted. "She didn't actually give me the wrong number."

"What? You just said she gave you the wrong number."

"I *dialed* the wrong number."

Michael and Evan looked at each other suspiciously and laughed at Jody's expense.

"You sure this girl even exists?" Evan asked.

"You saw her last night. The girl I was talking to when you came over and grabbed me and told me to get up on the stage with Michael. The girl in the white dress."

"Who? I must have missed her."

They met at a cafe in Manhattan at 7 p.m. Shelly had arrived before Jody, and for the first time he could remember, he felt nervous. Was this a good sign? Maybe he felt this way because he wanted it to work. He walked through the door and toward the back, looking around for her. It was an ordinary cafe with sandwiches and coffees and a small deli case with pastries—so ordinary, in fact, that it wouldn't've been plausible in a movie.

"What are you looking for?"

Jody knew it was her voice before he turned around to greet her.

Shelly stood there behind him.

"What?"

"What are you looking for?" she asked again.

He turned around and faced her. "I'm looking for eternity. Will you find it with me?" Why was he saying these ridiculous things?

She giggled and looked down bashfully.

"Do you always wear that white dress?"

"We're sitting over there," she said and led him to their table.

The evening sun burned through the front windows and casted long shadows onto everything. Shelly was facing the storefront, bathed in daylight, the sun's rays tangled with her face.

They walked to their table and their shadows held hands even though they weren't touching. Her small frame was twice its height when cast backward onto the floor. They sat at their table and she said nothing with words—she didn't have to. And within a few moments, any trace of lingering dismay that Jody'd felt had dissipated.

"Is that your journal?" she asked, pointing at his notebook on the table.

"This? Sort of. I mean, you know, if songs are journal entries, then, yeah, this is my journal."

She flipped it open without asking whether it was alright. "Looks like you write in Arabic," she said. commenting on his handwriting.

"That's just so other people can't read the lyrics."

"Do you carry this notebook everywhere?"

"I used to, and then I stopped for a few years. But I was helping my friend write some songs today. Michael—the guy from the concert last night—he's recording an album."

"That's great," she said. "What's this song about?" She pointed at his chicken scratch on the page.

"I'm not always sure what they're about, but this one I have a pretty good idea: I think it's about some half-hearted attempts to fix my problems—while the other half of my heart runs and hides. Or something like that. You know: love and loneliness—the key ingredients of any good song, right?"

"Love *and* loneliness?"

"Without love, a song is just a cry for help. It's a thousand-ton freight train with no cargo."

"But doesn't loneliness make it a *sad* song."

"Sometimes love *is* sad. Sometimes it drops your heart from a great height and it shatters into a million tiny shards, and those shards are sharp and painful."

Shelly flipped the page, looking for something less dark. "What's that line say?" she pointed and asked.

"Umm, you know it's kind of embarrassing to talk about it like this. Plus if you just read lyrics out loud they can sound a little crazy."

"Don't be silly. I'm not going to judge you. What's it say?"

"OK. It says, 'Hold on, this will hurt more than anything ever has before.'"

"Another love song?" she asked and shut the notebook.

"Something like that."

"Do any of your songs end happily?"

"I think so. Love or lust or whatever you want to call it is a complicated thing. Sometimes it doesn't end at all—sometimes it just lingers and overlaps and intersects with other fragments of love. Sometimes it does end, and we don't even know it has ended until after it's over. But I don't know whether it ever ends happily as in *happily ever after*. I don't know whether it works that way. But now I'm just babbling and probably making no sense at all."

"No, I'm following you. I don't necessarily agree with you, but I'm following what you're saying."

"I look at it like this: love wins, but love also *ends*, and when it ends it's painful. So *winning*—at least a part of winning—is painful."

"Or maybe you can find a way to turn that pain into pleasure," she said. "Maybe the pain is necessary to gain the pleasure. Maybe you can't have one without the other. Life—and love—doesn't work without both. They *are* both. And so by avoiding pain, you're actually avoiding pleasure."

Jody liked what she was saying. He wasn't used to participating in deeper conversations with women he dated, but he liked it. "You're not going to believe me, but I had a dream about you the other night."

"About me?"

"Yes. And in that dream you said basically the same thing you're saying now. And you said this one line, a line that stuck with me—you said 'You can't get around what you have to go through.'"

"Interesting. Maybe it wasn't a dream—" she was interrupted by the waiter, a burly man with hairy arms asking to take their order. They both ordered the same exact thing, which felt strange but just right for some reason. The conversation lightened as they ate. They spoke about Ohio, reciting niceties about their childhoods. She said she was headed back in a few days. He said he thought he was too. They both laughed at how

Jody had dialed the wrong number when he tried to call her, and she told him that she'd thought he must've forgotten about her. They spoke of their pasts, but for the first time Jody's past was beginning to feel like what it really was—a *past*, a time before all of this. Maybe he had finally earned his past.

After their meal, they exited into the New York twilight. Jody walked out of the cafe first, and he quickly shut the door behind himself, and now the glass door was the only thing between them. He held the door shut and stared at her through the glass. She was perfect. He fogged the window with his breath and drew a face on its pane and told her through the door that it was her face, and she smiled, not unlike the fading portrait on the glass.

Jody opened the door.

"Central Park isn't too far from here if you'd like to walk there," she invited him to join her. Jody agreed and they walked side by side without saying much, not for a lack of things to talk about, but because they enjoyed an imperfect kind of quiet, the occasional horn or car door or random street noise in the distance. They sat next to each other on an iron bench beneath a wrought-iron sky and its expectant moon. Jody enjoyed their time together, and he hoped more than anything that she did as well. They talked for hours in the park, but it seemed like only a few minutes, like no time at all had passed. Eventually they both knew when it was time to go. He wanted to find a way to go with her, for her to take him back to where she was staying, but he knew this wouldn't be possible. Girls like her didn't invite guys home after a first date. Was that what this was—a first date? *First* implies future dates, doesn't it? This thought made him happy, excited in some new way. Jody made sure he had her correct number this time, reciting it back to her several times, and he made sure she had his number just in case something went wrong. He promised to call her when he got back to Ohio. She told him she looked forward to getting to know him better. He wasn't entirely sure what this meant, but he liked it nonetheless. Before she left him, they hugged, and after they embraced, they both lingered that extra moment. He looked down upon her from a foot above. *Don't waste this kiss* her eyes said, looking up, looking for him to connect with her. They closed their eyes. Her closed lips were soft, tender.

As Shelly walked away Jody sat down on the bench again and watched her get smaller until she was a white dot in the distance. He remained on the bench for a while, taking it all in before walking two blocks and waiting twenty-five minutes for the bus back to Brooklyn. He stood next to two men who were either Haitian or Dominican and who spoke essentially no English or at least refused to speak English to him when he asked them how long they'd been waiting. The bus arrived not long after he asked. He tolerated the dark ride across the bridge, thinking of Shelly the entire time, and eventually the bus turned on Broadway and they were back in Bed-Stuy. The problem was that none of the buildings or signs looked even vaguely familiar at night, especially through the lens of tinted windows on the bus. A few stops on Broadway went by and soon Jody was the only white person on the bus. *Why is this bus so crowded after midnight?* At the next stop a young kid who was maybe twelve or thirteen got on the bus and sat across from him. He looked friendlier than any of the other patrons.

"Hey man, do you know where the Sutton Avenue stop is at?"

The kid removed his headphones from his ears. "Huh?"

"Sutton Avenue? Do you know where the Sutton Avenue stop is?"

He leaned forward, faced left, looked through the bus's front windshield. "Like maybe eight stops."

"Thanks."

The kid nodded and put his earbuds back in but removed them a few minutes later to tell Jody to signal for the bus to stop, a process he was completely unfamiliar with, and so the kid hit the little button for him.

Jody stepped off the bus and the nighttime brought with it a quiet darkness. He walked down Putnam Ave., thoughts tumbling. *I'm in Bed-Stuy Brooklyn at night and I'm alone.* He walked with a fake confidence, his right hand gripping his phone in his front-right pant pocket as if he might be carrying a handgun. People sat on the stoops of their dilapidated brownstones at this hour, sleepless in Brooklyn. They paid him no mind. He didn't exist. More than half the streetlights didn't work, and the half that did flickered in an off-tempo strobe, illuminating a different world. Not even a single word or head-nod from a passerby. He was a ghost walking among the living, unnoticed, a fly on a dead thing. A car alarm sounded somewhere out of sight, making its way through an immense web of distances. He wasn't sure what purpose car alarms served. Nobody flinched or paid it any attention. Nobody thought *Hey that's my car!* or *Quick someone call the cops!* People were just annoyed by car alarms. They always thought it wasn't their car and wished someone would turn that damn thing off.

I wish someone would turn that damn thing off.

There is something about the night that strips people of assurances, working into them, making them feel the thinness of everything around them. Everything becomes more vivid when someone is this aware of their surroundings. The lights get brighter. The sounds, sharper. The sky, deeper. The air holds the smell of violence and vulnerability.

Jody is only eight blocks from Michael's apartment now. If it were daylight, he could see it in the distance among the other identical dwellings. But it's too dark, and now he hears a new sound behind him—the rhythmic sound of footsteps faster than his own: tssht tssht, tssht tssht. Two sets of footsteps, four individual feet on the concrete behind him. Rubber soles' friction on the ground: tssht tssht, tssht tssht. His hand clutches the phone in his pocket with urgency. *I'll use this if I have to* is the vibe he hopes to emit. The nearest streetlight flickers as he passes underneath it and three shadows dance on a building's brick wall to the tempo of the strobe. Tssht tssht, tssht tssht. Jody picks up the pace until his footsteps mimic theirs. Tssht tssht, tssht tssht, tssht tssht. Six separate feet, his and theirs. Three heartbeats, one faster than the other two. And suddenly the air feels different. Death, or something like it, hangs in the atmosphere, looming above the tenements and the rooftops and in the aphotic sky above, a cross-grain of rapture, anticipation, and emancipation, the latter of which seems to be freedom, true freedom, the freedom of death, and he sees his childhood there, a place from which he once escaped has now found him here in Brooklyn. He endures the rush of blood to his head. His heartbeat in his ear begins to drown out the footsteps behind him. Three blocks from Michael's now, and less than three blocks from something awful. He hasn't known fear as an adult, and yet something like fear has wrapped itself around him now, so strangely and totally near. He can hear only his heartbeat, thumping loudly and continuously, the only real sound in the universe. It is so loud and overwhelming that he's certain the entire neighborhood can hear it too. A liquor store's neon glow teases him from the distance. One of the footsteps' owners says something inaudible to the other set of footsteps, but everything else is white noise, static in the night next to the pounding of his heart. The loudest sound in the world is no sound at all. It is hot and humid and he is sweating, his shirt soaked, front and back. He can taste copper in his own saliva as it dries and fails to replenish. Less than one block now. Together, three as one, moving in unison, a trio so close that they appear a trinity to some faraway imaginary observer. *In the name of the Father, the Son, and the holy ghost.* An unseen TV talks in the distance. Another string of words from one of the sets of feet. Heh-heh-heh. Laughter. *Fuck. This is it. This is where I die. Robbed and murdered a week from my twenty-ninth birthday in New York City, a few feet from my final destination.*

Your life and death are set in place, just waiting for you to keep the appointments. No fear in the moments just before your death, only serenity. The sound of your heartbeat moves into the background, outside you now, floating outside yourself, past your death and back again. Say a prayer if you know one. All sounds become intensely vivid, clear, crisp. The changing of things that were always the same. The wind produces a sound you've never heard before. The flicker of a streetlamp radiates an indescribable beauty. It feels unfair for you to witness such magnificence at a time like this. The night sky is grayer and lower and denser than you've ever experienced. You feel a droplet of rain mix with the sweat on your forearm, the coming of a storm, the washing away of a million sins. One breath after another. Countdown. This is it. The footsteps behind you create a drumroll to the inevitable. You remember a scripture you didn't know you knew. Isaiah 45:7. *I form the light, and create darkness. I make peace, and create evil. I the LORD do all these things.* You take in everything at once, appreciate all the gifts surrounding you. Turn around. Fight or flight. Keys between your fingers. Flight is not an option. Not today. You see the footsteps' owners—two hulking men—wearing an aura of apathy. They don't even notice you. They are close enough for you to discover they are worlds away. They walk right past you, one set of footsteps to the left, one set to the right, fading into oblivion under the pulse of intermittent streetlight. You stand there, frozen, a relieved panic feeding your existence. You've never felt more alive. Brooklyn is on the map, but you are not here.

LIFE IN THE REARVIEW

FILTER Magazine Cover Story
February 25, 2011
Interview by Stanley Dukes

Jody Grafton tried to kill himself less than a
year ago. But that was the past: a past Grafton
doesn't relish, a past he's reluctant to discuss,
because, as he puts it, "it doesn't exist
anymore."

Five years ago, Grafton's second album, *Out of
the Storm*, was well-received by critics and fans
alike, culminating in a hit single, an
international headlining tour, and a promising
future for the young singer-songwriter.

Then in 2007, at the dawn of the new year,
something strange happened: Grafton seemed to
fall off the face of the earth. He released a
third album, *Speaking of Ohio*, but after mediocre
sales and an unexpected restructuring at Geffen,
he was dropped from the label. It appeared that
his fifteen minutes had expired.

This was, however, just the beginning of an
unfortunate four-year downward spiral. Looking
back, Grafton recounts a classic, almost cliche,
troubled-artist story. He stopped making music at
25, and he took to the bottle to numb the pain.
Then his mother died and his marriage ended

uglily; he went broke and knocked-up a girl he was dating; and eventually he tried to kill himself at 28. But he was on a magnificent losing streak, and after the hospital successfully pumped his stomach, the suicide was a failure, too.

Grafton had hit rock bottom, his world was over — or so he thought. Last summer, a few months after his botched suicide attempt, he traveled to Brooklyn to help his friend, singer-songwriter Michael Emerson, finish writing his debut album, *After the Storm* (Tommy Boy). That album turned out to be a successful endeavor for Emerson, yielding three hit singles and a Grammy nomination for Best New Artist. Since Jody received the main songwriting credits on much of that album, he was inadvertently thrust back into the spotlight.

"I didn't expect much to come from that trip," Grafton confessed. "I just needed to get away from Ohio for a while. I felt like I needed to go away if I ever wanted to come back."

More important, Grafton wrote eight of the ten tracks from his new album, *As a Decade Fades*, during his voyage to Brooklyn. "It was the first music I'd written in over three years," he confessed during our interview. "It was also the best music I'd ever written. I just wrote about my past and all the things I'd been through over the last decade. It was like I had to get it on paper so I could let go."

The album is different from his past three albums' sparse, acoustic, musical arrangements, and its material has matured considerably. Grafton no longer appears to be a man stuck in the depths of depression. There are dark, disturbing moments on this album, but the listener is left with the feeling that those moments of wreckage are a glimpse in the rearview, and that there's open road and blue skies ahead.

Grafton is at his best on "Best Friend," one of the two songs he wrote after returning to Ohio: "I came home / you put my hand on your belly / The baby wasn't mine / didn't have the heart to tell me." The song addresses the unexpected love triangle between Grafton, his ex-girlfriend, and his now former best friend.

"Heartbreak drives a blue Ford Focus," Grafton half-joked while discussing this song's backstory. It turns out that, unbeknownst to Grafton, the pregnant girl he was dating was also sleeping with his best friend. After his short stint in Brooklyn, Grafton returned to Ohio and stayed by her side until she gave birth to a child who was clearly not his. "I've never been more shocked in my life," he said. "I was in the delivery room, waiting on my son to be born, and then I saw her give birth to a baby boy — a *black* baby boy."

The child ended up being a by-product of a short fling between his girlfriend and Grafton's best friend, Eric Wallace, who also played bass guitar on Grafton's first three albums. Suffice it to say, Wallace's presence is distinctly absent on Grafton's new album. "People don't know how to love the ones they love / until they disappear from their lives," Grafton belts out during the song's third verse, implying the loss of his best friend, a loss at the end of a long string of losses, including Grafton's father, mother, brother, wife, girlfriend, and potential child, as well as his career, his music, and eventually his will to live. "I had to lose it all before I was able to realize that it wasn't the world that was conspiring against me; it was me and my own behavior that had led me down that miserable path. And my deeds didn't go unpunished."

These days, when Grafton plays "Best Friend" on stage, he playfully mixes in Michael Jackson's "Billie Jean," having fun with MJ's line, "but the kid was not my son." Although he acknowledges he didn't possess the same jovial sense of humor after leaving the delivery room. "Things got pretty heated," Grafton admits before spilling a few surface-level details. "To be honest, when I found out [the baby] wasn't mine, I was startled and overwhelmed and angry all at the same time. How could my best friend do this to me? How could this girl — this girl who claimed she loved me — do this to me? Are these the types of relationships I need in my life? And is this the type of person *I've* become? I didn't want to be like them, but I knew that in many ways I already *was* like them, and something needed to change — *I* needed to change. I mean, I was already done with the relationship with the girl — I had already moved on to something that was much healthier for me — but I was prepared to take care of what was mine. I was ready to see it through, to make things right, to take responsibility for my actions. I was terrified to be a father, but I was going to be there for my son. And even though the kid wasn't mine, I realized that going forward, my actions needed to change if I ever wanted to be happy. I couldn't keep living the same way I'd lived for most of my twenties."

Perhaps Grafton's "something healthier" is alluded to on the new album's final track, "Girl in the White Summer Dress": "Lost man, Ohio / in the City looking to be found / You have to go through / what you can't get around."

Like Grafton's sudden reprisal, the success of *As a Decade Fades* is also an unconventional story of victory in the face of seemingly insurmountable odds. Grafton recorded the songs on his own and released them on the Internet for free without a record label's backing. "I had [my new manager] Wes put together a website and I just gave the music to anyone who wanted it." The album garnered 21,000 downloads in the first week, which turned into more than 2 million downloads in time, exposing Grafton to an entirely new audience, a bigger audience, allowing him to embark upon a nationwide tour, attracting the attention of record executives at several different labels. "I discovered I didn't need to wait around for someone else to do all the work for me," Grafton said of his new audience, his new platform, and his newfound Internet fame.

This tattooed troubadour turns 30 this year, and *As a Decade Fades* seems to articulate his newfound happiness — his recovery after the crash. He is a better man today than he was yesterday, but he is far from perfect. He acknowledges his failures, mistakes, and bad decisions: "I'm not a saint, and I certainly don't have it all figured out . . . but I've found a few ways I can be happy."

Jody Grafton is still a mixed bag. He is the epitome of a human being: nuanced and imperfect, the darkness and the light. His story is unique — marked by internal struggle and strife, entangled with triumph and joy — and yet his story is no different from anyone else's. He has loved, laughed, and grown over the last decade. But he has also hurt, damaged, and lied. Most of all, Grafton has lived, and for that he bears no regrets.

This year marks a new decade for Grafton, a decade of opportunity. Perhaps his thirties will bring forth a particular kind of levity, a serenity and calm. Or perhaps life isn't meant to contain these absolutes. Perhaps one must sit in the valley to see the beauty of the mountaintop, to appreciate his ascent, to live a purpose-filled life. And perhaps the key is not to live in the valley, but rather, to be aware of why you were there and prepare for the journey ahead.

Toward the end of our time together, I asked Grafton about a line from his song "Beyond the Bottom of a Glass." In that song, he sings in his signature baritone over a crestfallen piano, "Sometimes rock bottom is the finest place to be." Grafton explained this sentiment with optimism: "For me, that line speaks of opportunity and growth and of a bright future, irrespective of your current situation, whether it's good, bad, or somewhere in-between."

Whatever the case may be, one assumes that Grafton will embrace this new life, even though it "scares the shit out of" him at times. "It's the only life I have," he said. Indeed, it appears to be a beautiful and terrifying and wondrous life.

The songs on *As a Decade Fades* give the listener the same sense of optimism as Grafton the man — optimism after intense struggle, beginning with the album's timid opening line, "Are you sure you want to do this?" and ending with its heartening last: "You are not here."

ACKNOWLEDGEMENTS

SPECIAL THANKS TO the scores of people who helped with this book, including, but certainly not limited to, Chase Night, Shawn Mihalik, Patrick McCord, Austen Nelson, Jeff Hirz, Bryant Ferguson, Chase Snyder, Andre Kibbe, Paul Jarvis, Dave LaTulippe, Jeff and Marla Sarris, Thom Chambers, Eve Johnston, Radhika Morabia, Eric Lally, Benjamin Spall, Dan Grant, Aline Reynders, Jorg Jungerhans, Justin Lawless, Sam Lustgarten, Brett Steele, Lynda Laurendine, Jessica Williams, James Calle, and Virginia Allen. Thank you to my loved ones who saw me through the angst and agony and eventual satisfaction of writing these pages: Colleen, Stan, Colin, Sam, Jerome, Shawn, Ryan, Adam, and Keri. Many thanks to the musicians and writers whose thoughts, ideas, and words I borrowed (commandeered) in an effort to append their art and somehow, in some tiny little way, make it my own. And to you, the reader, thank you. I appreciate you. There are many more people I'd like to thank, but I just don't have the pages. I hope you understand.

—JFM

BOOKS BY JOSHUA FIELDS MILLBURN

NONFICTION

Essential

Minimalism

Everything That Remains

FICTION

As a Decade Fades

ABOUT THE AUTHOR

JOSHUA FIELDS MILLBURN is a bestselling author, writing instructor, and international speaker. He is best known as one half of *TheMinimalists.com*, where he and Ryan Nicodemus write about living a meaningful life with less stuff. His books include *Essential: Essays by The Minimalists*, *Minimalism: Live a Meaningful Life*, *As a Decade Fades: A Novel*, and *Everything That Remains: A Memoir*. He has been featured in the *New York Times*, *Wall Street Journal*, *USA Today*, *Time*, *Forbes*, *Boston Globe*, *San Francisco Chronicle*, *Chicago Tribune*, *Seattle Times*, *Toronto Star*, *Globe & Mail*, *Vancouver Sun*, *Village Voice*, *LA Weekly*, and many other outlets. Visit the author online at JoshuaFieldsMillburn.com.

71085679R00158

Made in the USA
Middletown, DE
29 September 2019